Mitch & Sea

CATHERINE ELIZABETH LAMBERT

Edited by Sarah Morgan and Patricia Field
Cover Design by Patricia Field

ANOTHER BOOK BY CATHERINE LAMBERT

Lost in a Sea of Mothers: Am I a Mother Yet?
A Memoir.

ACKNOWLEDGMENTS

I want to thank my husband, Larry, for supporting me, for encouraging me to write my first novel and for your help with self-publishing. Thank you Sarah Morgan and Patricia Field, my mother, for helping me edit my first novel. Thank you Mom, Larry and Jan Barbato for your feedback, it was most instructive and helpful in making my story believable. I want to give a special thanks to my mother for designing my book cover. Once again, you outdid yourself. Thank you to friends and family for your support and encouragement to keep writing.

CHAPTER ONE

As Sea Gallagher tried on the last wedding dress for the day, her minty gum popped out of her mouth when she leaned forward to pull up the beautiful gown. As it left her mouth, she watched it shoot out and fall onto the dress. She stared at it with wide eyes hoping it hadn't stuck to the fabric—but it had. She immediately regretted putting so much gum in her mouth that morning. She couldn't help herself, though. Sea had loved gum ever since she was a little girl. Blowing bubbles and making noise. It was irresistible for her. But today wasn't a day she should have indulged in such fun. She was now looking at an eight hundred dollar dress with gum on it. It kept sticking to the fabric as she attempted to pull it off. After a few minutes, she managed to remove half of it but what remained was still very noticeable. Sea started to panic.

Sarah, her big sister and matron of honor, was a few feet away looking at other dresses on the rack.

"Sarah, come here!" Sea whispered as loud as she could.

No response.

Sea waved her hand in the mirror hoping Sarah would see her. She finally caught her eye and Sarah turned around.

"What's wrong?"

"Come here! Look! I got gum on the dress!"

Sarah looked down and saw a wad of gum in the middle of the front skirting. She couldn't believe her eyes. Sarah started laughing.

"It's not funny!" Sea cried. "I can't pay for this. What am I going to do?"

Sarah tried to regain her composure but she couldn't stop laughing. "You're going to have to pay for it, is my guess. I don't think Dad would be happy to pay for an eight hundred dollar wedding dress with gum on it."

"You think!" Sea said sarcastically.

"Does it fit?" Sarah asked.

"I didn't put it on yet." Sea replied. "I didn't get a chance to."

"Well, see if it fits. Maybe you can add some bows to the front, to hide it."

Sea pulled on the dress. It fit perfectly, and she looked very beautiful in it, despite the blob of gum on the front. It was close to what her idea of the perfect wedding dress would be. When she finished changing, Sarah hung up the dress for her while Sea went to the front of the store to look at veils.

Out of the corner of her eye, Sea saw a man enter the store. She turned her head and saw that he was scruffy looking. He seemed out of place. He walked straight up to the woman behind the counter and shouted, "You'll never make a fool out of me ever again, you cheating whore!" He raised his arm. Bang! He shot the woman right in the head. After a few seconds, he turned around. Unaware of her presence when he walked in, the shooter was startled when he noticed Sea standing there.

The man was now staring at her. Terrified, Sea didn't know what to do. She couldn't think straight. The man had just killed someone right in front of her and now he was pointing the gun at her. Frozen with fear and disbelief, she couldn't move.

Bang!

Time seemed to slow down. She could hear the door open and close as the shooter left. Sea looked down and could see blood staining her jeans. Suddenly, her knees buckled and she collapsed.

Sarah, another patron and the only other sales person in the store ran to the front when they heard the man leave. The sales woman called 911. Sarah ran to her sister. She found her curled up in the fetal position. The sales woman couldn't look at or go near her co-worker. It was too gruesome. There was nothing to do for her. She was clearly dead.

Sarah understood that her sister was in serious trouble. She moved Sea's hand away from her abdomen so she could assess the situation. Sea was bleeding profusely, shivering and turning pale. Sarah had to act fast. She took off her sweater and pressed it against Sea's abdomen, hoping it would slow down the bleeding. Sarah prayed her sister would survive.

"Sea?" Sarah begged through her tears.

Sea didn't answer. She had passed out.

Sarah laid her sister's head in her lap and pleaded, "Hold on. You're going to be okay. I'm here. The ambulance is coming." Sarah continued to cry.

Although Sarah's husband, Maxwell Stone, and their two small boys kept her quite busy she always managed time for Sea. They lived only a few miles from each other and their parents. Best friends, they planned to raise their babies together.

The ambulance arrived along with the police. The seven minutes it took for the paramedics to arrive seemed like an hour for Sarah. She was so afraid of losing her baby sister—her best friend.

From a distance, Sarah heard the sales woman tell the police that the culprit was most likely her dead co-worker's husband. She confessed that she herself had called the husband earlier that morning to tell him what his wife was up to. She was acting very inappropriately for a married woman. Different men would pick her up from work or drop her off. His wife was defiling the sanctity of marriage and her co-worker couldn't keep quiet any longer. While the sales woman thought the husband should know, she had no idea he would do something that horrific.

The wronged husband was full of anger and hatred for all women at that exact moment—Sea was at the wrong place at the wrong time.

CHAPTER TWO

Sea's fiancé, Trevor Sullivan Jr., was pacing back and forth. "I can't believe this is happening. Who would do something like this? Why Sea? How long did they say the surgery would take? Why haven't we heard anything yet? God, let her be all right."

Mrs. Sullivan tried to calm her son down. "She's young and strong. The doctors are doing their best to save her. They will be out to talk to us as soon as they can."

Mr. Sullivan tried to calm him down as well. "Son, sit down, please. You'll wear yourself out. The doctors are well-trained here. She's in good hands."

"I can't sit down. What will I do without her?" Trevor's work shoes kept squeaking as he paced. "What if she doesn't make it? I love her so much, Mom." Trevor ran his fingers through his hair and started pacing again.

"I know you do son but you're going to drive yourself crazy. Come sit down," his mother said compassionately.

Trevor and Sea were high school sweethearts. He was a member of the debate team and she was the yearbook photographer. They met through a mutual friend and started dating during their junior year. His parents didn't approve of their relationship at first because they expected him to marry someone who was more sophisticated. Sea was down to earth and less worried about superficial matters. But over time, his parents grew to love and admire her. She was beautiful and smart and they felt she was capable enough to produce suitable offspring to carry on the family name. Trevor's only other sibling was a girl so they were counting on him.

Sea's parents, brother-in-law and nephews finally arrived at the hospital. The Sullivans briefed them on her condition and that she was still in surgery. Mr. Gallagher would have been there sooner but he had been an hour away painting a house. Mrs. Gallagher hadn't received the message until she had finished with her one o'clock appointment. A psychologist for twenty-five years, she was adamant about not being disturbed during sessions. Maxwell picked the boys up from school and headed toward the hospital as soon as he was able to leave work. Sarah was grateful and comforted to have her husband and children by her side.

Sea and Sarah were much closer to their dad than to their mother. Sea had invited her mother to go shopping with them but, as usual, her mother declined, blaming her busy work schedule. Sea was relieved but saddened that her mother didn't show any interest in helping with the wedding. The girls were nurtured more by their father, who had a flexible schedule. Five years older, Sarah had taken over as a mother figure for Sea at an early age, since their mother put far more energy and time into her career than into her children.

After two more hours, the doctor finally walked through the double doors and into the waiting room. Trevor stood up with anticipation.

"Sea is going to be fine." The doctor assured them. "She's being taken to the ICU. The bullet entered her lower abdomen, perforated her intestines and damaged her uterus. We had to resection three small segments of her intestines and remove her uterus. We were able to salvage both her ovaries.

"So she's going to be okay?" Trevor asked concerned.

"Yes. She's going to be just fine. It will take some time for her to fully recover though. She won't be able to eat any solid food for about a week."

"You removed her uterus?" Mrs. Sullivan asked in disbelief.

The doctor gave her a grim look. "Yes. I'm afraid so Mrs. Sullivan."

Trevor slumped down in his chair. He was relieved that Sea would be okay but devastated to know that in order for him to have a family with Sea he would have to dish out a lot of money and time in order to have one child.

"I can't believe this." Sarah said. "My sister is going to be devastated. She wants to be a mother someday. Sea was telling me just yesterday how much she was looking forward to being a mother. We were going to raise our kids together. Who's going to tell her?"

"I was planning to tell her when she woke up," the doctor said. "If you'll excuse me I have another patient to attend to. You can go in and see your sister as soon as she wakes up."

Sarah was saddened by the news. She wanted her sister to have the same thing she did—a family of her own. She knew this would crush Sea. She began to cry softly for her sister's loss. Max took her into his arms and held her. Their two boys had been playing nearby but stopped when they saw their mother crying and walked over to hug her.

"Thank you, doctor," Mr. Gallagher said when the doctor walked away. Mrs. Gallagher didn't react much at all. She didn't want to see her daughter in pain but felt that there was more to life than raising children. "Her life isn't over. She can go to college and get a degree. She can find happiness pursuing a meaningful career."

"Shut up, Mom," Sarah said, annoyed. "Sea doesn't need to hear that. She wanted children. Try to have a little compassion. I know that may be hard, but do try."

"No need to be rude, Sarah," her mother chided.

"Why not? You don't even care about me or Sea. You didn't even want children. You didn't even make the time to go dress shopping with us. Most mothers would have been thrilled but you'd rather work. Who does that?"

"Sarah. That's no way to talk to your mother. This is a difficult time for everyone," her father scolded.

Sarah quieted down and Mrs. Gallagher left for a moment to get coffee.

Mr. Sullivan looked up from his magazine and saw two detectives asking a nurse where the Gallagher family was. He walked over to where they were standing to point them in the right direction.

"Are you Mr. and Mrs. Gallagher?" Detective Diaz asked.

They both turned around as the detectives approached. "Yes, we are."

Everyone else gathered around to hear what the detectives had to say.

"My name is Detective Maria Diaz and this is my partner Detective Gil Albertson. We have been assigned to your daughter's case."

"Did you catch the guy yet?" Mr. Gallagher asked.

"Not exactly. When we arrived at the suspect's home, we found that he had committed suicide. To close this case though, we would like your daughter to identify him from a photograph. From what the patron and the sales woman say back at the bridal gown store, Sea is the only one who actually saw his face. Before we can close the case, we want to make sure that this is the man who shot her."

Sarah spoke up first. "Yes, that's right. I was hanging up her dress in the changing room and the other two women were in the back of the store talking."

"What did you hear?" Detective Albertson asked.

"I heard the front door open and someone walk in. A man shouted something and a second later I heard a gunshot and someone falling to the floor. I was too scared to look so I stayed out of sight until I thought the shooter was gone. Then I heard another shot. Soon after the door opened the shooting stopped, so I assumed it was the shooter who had left. I didn't see anything. As soon as I felt it was safe, I went to the front of the store to check on my sister. That's when I found her on the floor."

"Sea is out of surgery, but when she wakes I'm sure she wouldn't mind talking to you if she's able." Mr. Gallagher offered.

"Thank you, Mr. Gallagher. Please call us when she does." Detective Diaz handed him her card.

*

At about nine o'clock the next morning, Sea finally awoke. She grimaced from the pain in her abdomen and was now more alert. She noticed Sarah sleeping in the chair beside her.

"Sarah!" Sea barely managed to get out. "Sarah!" She tried again. Sarah finally awoke. "What is it? You okay?"

"What happened?" It was difficult for Sarah to make out her words since Sea's throat was still hoarse from the intubation.

"You were shot in the abdomen. The sales clerk at the bridal gown store was shot by her jealous husband—or so everyone thinks—and for some reason shot you as well. The police will be by later to ask you to identify who you saw. They are going to bring a picture of the husband."

"I remember now." Sea said. "It was horrible Sarah. It was so surreal to watch another human being die like that."

"I bet." Sarah replied. "I was so scared that I would lose you. You almost died in my arms."

"I seem to be fine now. I'm not going anywhere if I can help it."

"What hospital am I in?" Sea asked.

"You're at St. Matthew's Medical Center in Annapolis. It was the closest one to the store." Sarah answered.

"Where are Mom and Dad? Does Trevor know I'm here?" Sea asked.

"I'm not sure where Mom and Dad are. I've been asleep for a while. I'll call them in a few minutes. Trevor was the first one to the hospital. I think he broke every traffic law. He was here about fifteen minutes after I called him which was right after we arrived in the ambulance. He was here all night at your bedside but I told him to go home and get some sleep. He will be back in a few hours. I've already been home. I was able to get in a few hours of sleep, shower, and come back here to relieve Trevor. And be with you of course. Trevor has been taking this hard."

"Taking what hard?" Sea asked. "I'm going to be okay, right?"

"Yes, of course." Sarah quickly assured her. "It's just that there's more to your situation that you haven't been told yet."

"Like what?"

"The doctor will be in later to talk to you. He should be the one to tell you."

"Tell me what? If you know something Sarah, you need to tell me."

Just then, their parents walked in.

"Hey, sweetheart."

"Hi, Dad. Hi, Mom."

"How are you feeling? I was worried about you. You slept for a long time." Mr. Gallagher said as he walked over to give his daughter a kiss on the cheek. Mrs. Gallagher gave her a kiss on the cheek after her husband did but didn't say anything.

"I'm a bit sleepy and sore but okay. I'm glad you're here."

"Of course I'm here. I was worried about my girl. I thought I might lose you." Mr. Gallagher got misty eyed. He was dreading the other news she would soon learn.

"I'm fine Dad. I'll be good as new in a few weeks."

A hushed silence enveloped the room. Sarah looked at her dad for a signal as to whether or not she should say anything.

"What's going on? Why is everyone acting so funny? I'm not a child. I can handle whatever it is you need to tell me."

"I don't think you can my dear," her mother said.

"What's that supposed to mean?" Sea said in distress. "What's going on? Sarah? Dad?"

Sarah and her dad looked away. They couldn't face her.

"Oh, for heaven's sake, you can't have children. That's what everyone is so afraid to tell you. If you ask me though, I don't think it's so terrible. Now you can go to college and pursue a career." Motherhood never made her happy in life and she wanted to spare her daughter the suffering she went through. To her, being successful was much more fulfilling than being a mother.

"What do you mean I can't have children?" Sea said in disbelief.

"Mom! Why do you have to be so heartless?" Sarah said with contempt. "Sea has been through enough. She doesn't need to listen to you lecture her about school. Just because you hated motherhood doesn't mean Sea and I will. I have two wonderful boys and I can't imagine my life without them."

"You think Sea wants to hear that either?" her mother mocked. "I'm sure she doesn't want to hear you rubbing it in her face that you can have children. How thoughtless, Sarah. Really."

Sarah rolled her eyes.

Mr. Gallagher was displeased with his wife's attitude. "Evelyn, stop! Sea needs her family's support, not you two bickering."

Evelyn sighed and didn't say anything else.

Sea's mind was swirling. She began to doubt what she was being told. "How do you know I can't have children?" she asked.

"The doctor said so, Honey," her father answered. "Evelyn, explain it to her please."

From a distance, her mother looked her in the eyes and said, "The doctor had to remove your uterus. It was too badly damaged to repair. You still have both your ovaries, so if you want a child, the only way will be through a surrogate."

Sea was taken aback. "I can't believe this. There's no way. Surrogacy is too expensive."

"He also said that you wouldn't be able to eat solid food for about a week. Your intestines were damaged as well. I'm sure the doctor will be in to tell you everything in more detail but I thought you should know," her mother added.

"I'm so sorry sweetheart. I wish there was something I could do to make you feel better," her father said somberly.

Sea started to cry.

Mrs. Gallagher became uneasy. She didn't like being around people who were crying. "We'll leave you with your thoughts. I'm sure there's a lot for you to digest. Just remember, your life isn't over. There is so much more life can offer you besides being a parent."

Mr. and Mrs. Gallagher got up from their seats and said their goodbyes. "I'll drop by tomorrow after work, sweetheart. I love you!" her dad said.

"I'll keep you company, Sea. You shouldn't be alone."

"I think Mom and Dad had the right idea, Sarah. I want to be alone for a while."

Sarah didn't want to leave her sister's side. "Are you sure you want me to leave too? If you want, I can go get some of your favorite food and bring it back. That would cheer you up. You must be starving."

"I can't have solid food, remember? I'm not hungry anyway. Just go away! I want to be alone."

Sea was agitated and her machines where going off because she was getting so upset. A nurse ran in to calm her down.

"What seems to be the matter? What's going on?" the nurse asked.

"My sister won't leave. I want to be alone," Sea answered her.

"Your sister needs her rest, Mrs. Stone. You can come back tomorrow."

Sarah walked over and sat on the bed next to Sea. "If there's anything I can do, name it. We'll get through this."

"We'll? Your life wasn't turned upside down—mine was." Sea looked away.

"Please leave, Sarah. I want to be alone! Go!"

Nurse Robertson came to Sea's rescue. "You really need to leave now Mrs. Stone. I'm going to give your sister a sedative to help her sleep."

"I'll be back tomorrow, Sea." Sarah was in tears as she left.

CHAPTER THREE

Trevor was back at Sea's bedside later that afternoon. He wanted to talk to her the minute she awoke. He hadn't been able to sleep much while he was at home. He hadn't eaten since the moment he found out. Trevor called work to ask for another day off. He was a wreck. He was deciding whether or not he wanted to be with someone who was infertile, or to break off the engagement. He couldn't imagine his future without Sea in it. She was his high school sweetheart. He loved her but he wanted a family of his own as well. He didn't want to spend all of his hard earned money on fertility treatments and surrogacy. He really wanted to make a family the old fashioned way. He was torn.

As Trevor waited for Sea to awaken, he debated whether or not to move forward with the wedding. He kept pacing, trying to figure out the right words to say to her. He knew that she had been through so much and he didn't want to hurt her any more than she already was. The guilt was eating him alive. What would he say? How would he tell her?

As Sea was stirring and about to open her eyes, the detectives walked in. Trevor would have to wait a little longer. He stopped pacing and sat down.

"Good afternoon, Miss Gallagher." Detective Albertson said. "Do you think you're up to answering a few questions for us?"

"I guess so." Sea replied as she tried to sit up. She answered all of their questions to the best of her knowledge and positively identified the clerk's husband as the shooter from a photograph they showed her.

Detective Diaz stood up from her chair and said, "Thank you Miss Gallagher. We will let you know if we need anything else, but for right now, it sounds like an open and shut case. You have a good day now."

Trevor stood up and walked over to Sea's bed. She could tell that something was wrong. He wouldn't look at her.

"Are you okay, Trevor?" Sea asked.

"No... I'm not, Sea. I have something to tell you. This is very difficult for me to say but..." He hesitated. Trevor was having a difficult time getting the words out. His mouth was dry and pasty.

"But... what? You're starting to scare me Trevor. What's going on?" Sea insisted.

Trevor hesitated for another moment. He finally mustered up the courage to tell her. "I love you Sea... but I can't marry you. I want children someday and now that things have changed... I can't go through with the wedding. I'm sorry."

He gave her a minute to absorb his words.

Sea motioned for him to come over to the bed. She took his hand into hers.

"Don't be silly Trevor, we can still have children. It may take longer and more money but we can do anything we set our minds to. We can even adopt if we choose to." Sea assured him. "We can do this. It will be an adventure."

"I want children the old fashioned way, Sea. I also want the Sullivan blood line to continue. My parents are counting on me. It may have been different if I had a brother but I don't. And I don't want to raise someone else's kid. I've been thinking about this all night. I've barely slept or eaten in the last twenty-four hours. I don't want to hurt you Sea but we can't get married." Trevor moved his hand away.

"If you don't want to hurt me, then don't do this, Trevor," Sea said, as she tried to understand what was happening. She couldn't take it all in.

"I need you now more than ever. You are my fiancé and you said you loved me. You said you wanted to spend the rest of your life with me. Don't be selfish Trevor." Sea was desperately trying to save her relationship. She loved him so much.

"It wouldn't be fair to me or to you, Sea. I wouldn't be happy spending all of my time, energy and money endeavoring to create a family that wouldn't even be a guarantee and I definitely wouldn't want to adopt."

Sea looked away in disbelief. Everything was happening so fast. Her life was spiraling out of control. Her future was looking bleaker by the moment. She yearned for his support.

Sea looked at Trevor again. "I love you! Don't do this! Plenty of people go through fertility treatments or try to adopt. There are so many kids that need to be adopted. It would be a good thing for us. We would make great parents to a child that needed a loving home."

"I'm sorry Sea, but I can't. I wouldn't be happy. That's not the kind of life that I want."

"How can you abandon me now? After all I've been through. We love each other and that should be enough."

He couldn't meet her eyes anymore and looked down.

"I'm very sorry, Sea. I just can't. Please forgive me." Trevor started to collect his things and headed toward the door.

Sea quickly responded. "Well… I'm not going to call all of our friends and family to tell them there is no wedding. You can!" she said angrily.

She began to cry.

"I'll take care of all the cancellations and I'll pay whatever deposits your father had already made. I'll mail you a check next week." Trevor walked over to her bed and bent down to give her a kiss on the cheek. Sea didn't respond. He walked to the door, turned, and said, "Goodbye, Sea."

Sea didn't say anything as he walked away. She knew it was futile. It wasn't fair to him or to her. Sea continued to cry.

Sea told the nurse that she didn't want any more visitors for the day.

CHAPTER FOUR

Sea was discharged from the hospital two weeks after the shooting. She called her father to come pick her up. She wasn't in the mood to talk to her sister. Sea waited patiently for her father to come by on his lunch break. Not much was said on the drive home. He helped her out of the car and brought her bags to her bedroom.

"Thanks for bringing me home Dad." Sea said, as she gave him a hug.

"You are most welcome sweetheart. Call me if you need anything. And remember, don't be lifting anything too heavy, like the doctor said."

"I won't. I promise. I love you and have a great day," she said.

"I love you too. See you soon."

Sea was surprised to find that someone had cleaned her apartment and stocked her refrigerator. Her first thought was that Trevor had changed his mind and wanted to make it up to her by cleaning her place. Could it be true? As she was about to dial his number, she heard a knock on the door. It was Sarah.

"Hey Sis. How are you feeling?"

"I'm okay, still a bit sore though."

"Do you like your surprise?" Sarah asked. "Dad called me this morning and told me you were going home today. I wanted to make sure you could relax when you got home so I came by earlier today to fix it up. Dad wanted me to keep an eye on you and be here if you needed anything."

"Oh. Thank you, Sarah, that was very nice of you." Sea said a bit deflated. She was really hoping it had been Trevor.

"I'm going to go lie down. Thanks again for your help, Sarah."

"No problem. Would you like me to fix you something to eat?"

"No… Not right now, thanks. I'm not hungry."

"Okay. Well let me know if you need anything. I'm going to fix myself some lunch. I'll be around for a while in case you change your mind."

"Okay. Thanks."

Sea's abdomen was still pretty sore so she went to her bedroom to lie down. When she entered the room, she saw a big brown box in the middle of the bed. She had no idea who sent it or what it could be. As she turned the box around, she could see that it was from the bridal gown store. She didn't remember purchasing anything so she was perplexed as to why it was there. On the inside was a note that read:

Dear Miss Gallagher,

My name is Pam Gunthrie. I am the owner of the bridal gown store you were injured in. I am so sorry that this awful incident happened to you in my store. I would like you to have this wedding dress I sent over as a token of my sincerest condolences to your condition. Also, I did see the dress you stained and I don't want you to worry about paying us back for that dress either. I do hope this wedding dress is to your liking and fits you properly. If not, you can bring it to our tailor and he will make sure you're well taken care of, free of charge. I hope your wedding is beautiful!

Best Wishes,

Pam Gunthrie, Owner

Sea didn't bother to take the dress out of the box to look at it. There was no point. She stuffed the note back into the box and threw the whole thing into the closet. Once it hit the floor, part of the dress slipped out. She waved it off. She wasn't going to wear it anyway.

"Why did you do that?" Sarah asked.

Sea jumped. "Sarah! You surprised me!"

"Sorry."

"I thought you were in the kitchen."

"No. I wanted to see your reaction when you saw the dress. I didn't mean to startle you. So… why did you throw the box into the closet?" Sarah asked. "I thought you would be putting on the dress by now."

"No. I don't feel like it. I'm still too sore." Sea said, annoyed.

"What?" Sarah exclaimed. "I thought you'd be excited. What's wrong?"

"Nothing's wrong." Sea said unconvincingly.

Sea didn't want Sarah to know she had been dumped by Trevor.

Not yet. She was too angry and embarrassed to talk about it. Too many conflicting emotions were whirling through her. Sea was in no mood to talk, especially with her seemingly perfect older sister. She could never have what Sarah had—a biological family. How could she confide in someone who had no clue what she was going through? She wanted to be left alone.

"You've never had a problem opening up to me before." Sarah complained. "I'm your sister. We tell each other everything."

"I know we do Sarah, but not this time. I want to be alone. Thanks for your help with everything—I really appreciate it. You're a good sister, but I need some space."

"You're welcome… but I disagree. You shouldn't be alone right now." Sarah insisted.

Sea was distressed. She knew Sarah meant well but Sea felt suffocated in her sister's presence. What she really wanted to do was scream into her pillow and curse God for what was happening to her.

"I'll be fine, Sarah. We will talk tomorrow. I'm not feeling very well and I need to go to bed now." Sea tried to ease her sister's mind.

Sarah said, "Okay. But. I'm going to stay until you fall asleep."

"Really! I'm fine! Go! Don't you have kids at home to take care of?"

"Max said he would watch them for me."

Sea was losing her patience. "Doesn't he work today?" she asked angrily.

"No, he has off today." Sarah answered, bewildered. "Today is Memorial day."

Sea was exasperated. She didn't want to hurt her sister's feelings but now she had no choice.

"Sarah!" Sea snapped. "I was hoping you would get the hint! I've tried to be nice about this but can you get the fuck out now! I want to be alone!"

Sarah's eyes grew enormous and tears started to stream down her face. Sea felt horrible but wanted to be alone more than anything.

"Sea, you've never talked to me like this before. What is wrong with you? Talk to me! Why are you acting so strange?" Sarah was desperate and would never forgive herself if she left her baby sister alone at a time like this.

"What is wrong with me?!" Sea shouted. "Oh, let me see! I was shot in the abdomen. I may never have children of my own. And not long after that, my fiancé breaks up with me. Are you satisfied now?!" she said fuming. "Now get out!" Sea pushed her sister back into the hall and shut the bedroom door in her face.

"I'm so sorry, Sea." Sarah said through the bedroom door.

There was no response.

Sarah continued to cry as she walked to the living room to collect her things. She felt horrible. She hated seeing her sister in so much pain. This was something she wasn't able to fix. All she could do for her was to leave her alone.

Sea felt awful. She hated how she behaved toward her sister but she wanted to be alone. Once she heard the front door close, she curled up onto her bed and started screaming into her pillow. When she finished screaming, she went to her medicine cabinet and poured a whole bottle of pills into her hand. She sat there and stared at them, feeling sorry for herself. After a while, she put them back into the bottle and went back to bed.

CHAPTER FIVE

Two months later, Sea and Sarah met at a café to talk. It had been hard for Sarah to stay away but she wanted to wait until her sister was ready. It was the longest the two sisters hadn't talked since Sea was born.

"It's great to see you Sarah." Sea said, as she embraced her sister. "Thanks for coming."

"It was short notice but I was able to find a sitter. I've been really worried about you and didn't want any distractions while we talked." They found a booth in a corner of the café.

Sea leaned over and whispered, "I'm sorry I cursed at you a while back. I felt I had no choice. My heart was aching and I was inconsolable. I really wanted to be alone."

Sarah hesitated. "You hurt me, Sea." she said disappointedly. "You've never shut me out like that before. I'm your sister. We should be able to tell each other everything."

The sisters were quiet for a few moments taking in what the other had said. The waitress came by and took their drink orders.

Sea said, "I couldn't talk to you about this because I was embarrassed. The man I loved left me. He didn't think I was worth staying for. That's so humiliating. You have no idea what I've been going through. You have two gorgeous kids of your own and a husband who loves and supports you. When I look at you now, it only reminds me of what I don't have."

Sea felt awkward around her sister now. It was hard to face someone whom you treated poorly and who seemed so perfect. Sarah had everything she ever wanted. Sea lost everything she ever wanted.

"Also, I asked you here because I wanted to tell you in person that I'm moving."

"You're moving! Why?" Sarah asked. "Why are you punishing me? I'm not the one who hurt you." Sarah was becoming angry and thought Sea was being irrational.

At that moment, the waitress walked up to the table to hand them their drinks. She could tell there was tension in the air so she quickly got their food orders and left.

"I'm depressed and hurting inside, Sarah. I need to get away from here. I need a fresh start somewhere else. I'm sorry you feel hurt by this but my life isn't all about you. You're a great sister and I love you, but I need this. It's too painful to stay. I can't be around you right now. It only reminds me of what I don't have. It took all of my strength to keep from hurting myself these past two months. I came close a couple of times."

"What stopped you?"

"I knew how much it would hurt you and dad. I couldn't do it."

"What about your job?"

"I hate my job and my co-workers are complaining about me because they always have to pick up my slack. I've been so depressed lately that it's been difficult to concentrate at work. And I've been written up twice already."

A tear streamed down Sea's face.

Sarah listened. There was nothing she could say to make her sister feel better.

"There is something you can do, Sis. Support my decision to leave. Don't be mad. Forgive me for yelling at you. I'm truly sorry."

"You know I could never stay mad at you, Sea. You're my baby sister. I understand how upset you were that night and I have already forgiven you for it. I love you."

Sea smiled. "Thanks, Sarah. I love you too."

Sarah hesitated before she asked her next question, "If you don't mind me asking, have you thought about seeing a therapist?"

"I did for a while, but it didn't help much because every morning on my way to work I have to drive by the bridal shop. Every morning I'm reminded of what happened to me and how it's changed my life." Sea replied. "I didn't see the point of it anymore. Maybe I'll start up again once I've settled in a new town."

Sarah nodded her head in agreement. "That makes sense. It's too hard to start over and heal when you're reminded every day of what happened."

"Exactly."

"Where are you going to go?"

"I'm going to Northampton to move in with Aunt Bridget. Dad mentioned she could use some help in her studio. It would be the perfect opportunity for me. Mom wasn't thrilled about the idea, but she'll get over it."

The waitress came by with their food.

Sea continued. "I think it will be good for me. I've given two weeks' notice at work. I went online and found a part-time job for the days Bridget won't need me."

"This is really happening."

"Yes. But I will visit as often as I can."

"You better." Sarah teased.

Sea couldn't wait to get away.

CHAPTER SIX

"It's great to see you Sea," Aunt Bridget said. "Make yourself at home. I was about to make some tea. Would you like some?"

"No thanks." Sea replied. "I'm going to bed early. I'm exhausted. I've been driving all day and I have an early interview in the morning."

"Okay. We can catch up tomorrow."

"Great. Thanks for letting me live here, Aunt Bridget. I really needed to get away."

"No problem, my dear. Glad I could help."

Sea hugged her aunt goodnight and made her way up the stairs to the guest bedroom.

*

Sea rolled onto her side and caught a glimpse of the time. Her eyes opened wide when she realized she had overslept. Her interview was in an hour and it took fifteen minutes to get there. Sea panicked. She dashed out of bed and into the shower. If she didn't hurry, she was going to be late. She tried to wash herself as fast as possible. She still had to iron her clothes. Because Sea was in such a rush she kept dropping the soap and the shampoo bottle slipped out of her hand and fell on her big toe. She yelped when it hit. Sea was in the shower less than ten minutes. She quickly ironed her clothes, put her make-up on and pinned up her hair. When she was finished, she grabbed her purse and went downstairs. Aunt Bridget had some toast waiting for her.

"Thanks Auntie. You're a life saver," she said, as she grabbed it from the plate.

"Good luck!" her aunt yelled out, as Sea vanished around the corner and out the door.

*

"Wait! I'm going up! Please hold the door!" Sea shouted. The man in the elevator quickly stretched out his arm to keep the door from closing.

"Thank you so much. I'm running late." she said, as she quickly dashed into the elevator.

He gave her a shy smile and then looked away. She noticed that he was wearing a gaming t-shirt and sneakers and looked extremely out of place. He had brown hair—what he had left of it, that is—and a stocky build. She also noticed his smile, it was warm and friendly. He looked roughly twenty-six to twenty-eight years old. Rather old to still be wearing gaming t-shirts, she thought. Sea smiled back at him as she pulled out her lipstick. Afterwards, she straightened out her clothes and took a deep breath to calm herself before she had to go in for her interview.

Out of the corner of her eye she could see that the man was staring at her.

"Is this your first day?" he asked.

Sea shook her head and said, "No. I have an interview on the eighth floor."

"Oh. Is that with Mr. Bennett or Mr. Gordon?"

"Mr. Bennett." she replied. "Do you know everyone who works here?"

"No, just a few," he answered.

"Do you work here?" she asked.

"No. I'm going up to the tenth floor to see my father. He used to work for Mr. Gordon."

The elevator door opened. Sea gave him a slight wave of her hand and whispered, "Bye" as she motioned to leave.

"Good luck," he called, as she stepped out of the elevator.

"Thanks!" Sea yelled, as she picked up her pace.

The man hesitated for a moment, "Can I get...?"

The gaming t-shirt man was not quick enough. Sea was fast on her toes and was down the hall before he could finish his sentence. He missed his opportunity. The elevator doors closed before he knew it. He was too caught up in the moment to remember what he had been doing before he met her. He wrapped his hand around the back of his neck, nervous, debating whether or not to go back to get her number. He didn't think he had much of a chance. She was nice enough but he doubted that this beautiful woman would give him the time of day. She had gorgeous red hair and blue eyes, and a nice physique. Surprisingly, he felt at ease in her presence. She wasn't putting on airs or full of herself. She seemed real to him. Almost like she didn't know how beautiful she was. It was the only reason he felt he might have a chance with her.

*

Sea's interview went along smoothly. Mr. Bennett said he would call her back in two days, if she got the job. He still had to interview a couple more people before making his final decision. Even though Sea was frazzled at first, she felt pretty confident that she got the job.

When Sea walked back to her car, in the garage, she noticed that one of her tires was flat. She let out a great big exasperated sigh and threw up her hands. Sea kicked off her heels and grabbed the spare tire and jack out of the trunk.

"Ow! Shit!" she cried out.

"Are you okay?" someone asked from a distance.

Sea turned around to see who it was. She recognized him. It was the gaming t-shirt man.

"Yeah. I'm fine. I broke a nail. I had them done a few days ago. I think I'll live."

"Do you need some help? I can change the tire for you, if you'd like." he offered.

Sea stood up. "Yes. Thank you. I'd appreciate that. I really don't want to ruin my nice clothes or break any more nails."

"Do you know how to change a tire?" he asked her, as he started rotating the handle on the jack.

"Yes. My ex-fiancé showed me how, last year. He thought it would come in handy someday. I guess he was right."

The man was thankful she had already placed the jack underneath the car because he didn't know anything about cars and especially how to change a tire.

"I really appreciate this. My name is Sea, by the way, and yours is?" The gaming t-shirt man stopped what he was doing to address her. He stood up and dusted the dirt off his hands. He extended his right hand and said, "My name is Michael Anderson but my friends call me 'Mitch'."

He then went back to jacking up the car.

"Why do they call you Mitch?" Sea asked.

"My best friend, Tommy, thinks I look like Mitch Pileggi from, 'The X-Files'."

"What are X-Files?"

"What's 'The X-Files'? You have to be joking. It's a huge cult classic television show from the 90's. I started watching it with my dad when I was 10. It was on for nine seasons."

"Ummm... isn't the tire too far off the ground now?"

"Don't worry, I got this." Mitch said, as he tried to unscrew the first bolt from the tire. After a few minutes, he wasn't making any progress. The tire kept spinning.

Sea started to giggle under her breath. She watched him try to hold the tire still as he attempted to unscrew the bolt. He wasn't getting anywhere.

"You've never changed a tire before have you?" Sea asked, as she chuckled aloud.

"No… not really." Mitch answered, as he started to laugh too. "I wanted to impress you, but I think that plan has backfired."

"You think?" Sea giggled some more. "You need to jack up the tire high enough so the weight of the car doesn't prevent you from removing the bolts but low enough so it's still slightly touching the ground so the tire won't move while you take the bolts off."

Mitch started lowering the jack.

"So why did your parents name you the letter 'C'?" Mitch asked, as he looked back at her.

"It's not the letter 'C' but 'Sea' like the ocean. My father loved to paint pictures of the sea when he was younger."

"Oh, I see." They both chuckled at the pun.

Mitch found it strange how easy it was to talk to her. "I'm surprised that you let me help you."

"Why is that?" she asked.

"Pretty women don't usually give me the time of day."

Sea looked at him and smiled. "I'm not like most women and I didn't feel like changing a tire, especially in these clothes. They're very uncomfortable."

Mitch laughed slightly and said, "Then why are you wearing them?"

"They look nice. I like wearing fashionable clothes. They usually end up being very uncomfortable though. Like these damn heels. They look amazing but kill my feet. But I can't not wear them."

"Okay. Whatever you say." Mitch shook his head. He didn't understand why women would torture themselves to look nice.

"You seem like a nice guy. If you dressed a little nicer, I bet more women would look your way. A man that's almost thirty wearing gaming t-shirts isn't exactly a babe magnet... no offense."

"None taken."

After another thirty minutes, Mitch got the donut put on and the jack down.

"Thanks so much for your help, Mitch."

"No problem. I didn't mind." They shook hands, but Mitch held on a little too long so Sea had to withdraw her hand. Mitch was about to speak again as she was getting into her car, but then changed his mind. He waved to her as she drove away.

Mitch walked over to his car and started to open the door, but hesitated. He really liked Sea. He wanted to see her again. He took a deep breath and puffed out his chest while gaining courage. "I can do this. Don't be such a wuss, Mitch." he said out loud to himself. He closed his car door then ran after her. He caught up to her car at the ticket booth and knocked on her passenger-side window. Sea jumped. Mitch smiled and motioned for her to put the window down. After she paid for the ticket, she hit the power button to lower the window. When Mitch saw that she was giving him her full attention, his anxiety rose. His mouth went dry and he couldn't speak clearly.

"I... ummm."

"Is everything okay, Mitch?" Sea asked.

Mitch looked away and side to side, "Yeah, everything is fine... it's just."

"Mitch?" she chuckled. "I'm holding up traffic. What is it that you wanted to say?"

He patted the top of her car and said, "Drive safe!"

"You knocked on my window to tell me to drive safe?" she asked.

He answered her with a half-smile, "Yeah… since you're driving home with a donut on. I wanted to make sure you got home safely."

"Thanks for your concern Mitch, but I really have to go now. Bye!" Sea put her hand up to tell him bye and to back away from the car. She pushed the power button and the window went up and cut Mitch off mid-sentence.

"Okay! Bye! Drive sa…!" Mitch shook his head and wanted to kick himself for being such a coward. "I'm such an idiot!" Mitch said under his breath, as he watched her exit the garage.

Sea looked straight ahead as she drove out of the parking garage and at the same time cringed from what she just experienced. She thought he was nice enough but a bit awkward.

CHAPTER SEVEN

"I thought you would've been back hours ago, Sea." Aunt Bridget said, as Sea walked in the front door. "It's past two o'clock and I have to leave soon. I won't be able to show you what I need done until tomorrow. I have a doctor's appointment at three this afternoon. Where have you been all morning?"

"Sorry I'm so late. I had a flat tire." Sea replied. "Someone helped me put the spare on and then I had to go get a new one. There were a few people ahead of me at the tire store so I had to wait a long time. It wasn't all bad though. I met someone."

"You met someone already?" her aunt said, surprised. "You just got here yesterday."

"I know. It's crazy. A cute guy at the tire store asked me out and he'll be here at eight to pick me up."

"Wow! I didn't think you'd be ready to start dating again."

"I know. Me neither. But, he is really sweet and easy on the eyes. I think you'll like him."

"I look forward to it," her aunt said, still looking a bit stunned.

Three months was long enough to get over losing a fiancé, she supposed. "Well I'd better go get ready. I'll be back in an hour or so. There's a man coming over to fix my computer at four. Please let him in if I'm not back yet."

Once her aunt left, Sea went to lie down on the couch. She was tired from her busy day so far and wanted to rest before her big date. Before she drifted off, she thought about all the things that had happened to her lately. She had moved to a new city and state. She was looking forward to spending time with her favorite aunt. Her job interview had gone well. Her confidence was lifted now that someone had asked her out. It had been three and a half months since Trevor broke off their engagement. It was time to move on with her life. She was beginning to feel happy again.

Knock! Knock! Knock! Sea jolted awake. She couldn't believe she had slept for an hour already. It was four o'clock on the dot. "I'm coming! Be there in a second!" Sea put on her shoes and quickly walked over to open the front door. When she opened the door, she became confused.

"You? What are you doing here?" Sea couldn't believe her eyes. "Are you following me?" She closed the door half way.

"No!" Mitch said indignantly. "I'm here to fix Bridget's computer. I had no idea you lived here. May I come in?"

Sea put it all together in her head and changed her attitude. "Of course. Sorry. Come in." Sea gestured for him to enter. "I'm sorry I was rude. I was confused. Forgive me. It's nice to see you again, Mitch. Thanks again for helping me this morning."

"You're welcome. I guess I can't blame you for being confused. I can only imagine how it looked at first. Plus, I was acting a bit strange this morning. Sorry about that. Beautiful women make me nervous."

"You didn't run after my car in the parking lot to tell me to 'drive safe', did you?"

Mitch winced. "No. I didn't."

"What was it then?" Sea asked playfully.

Mitch walked over to the computer to start working. He was trying to avoid the question. "You seem like a smart person. I'm sure you could figure it out." Mitch said in a playful manner.

"You were going to ask me out, weren't you?"

"How did you ever guess?"

"I have a sense about these things."

"Guys must hit on you all the time."

"Not all the time but sometimes. Someone from the tire store asked me out actually. We're going out on a date tonight."

"I'm not surprised." There was complete silence after he spoke. Sea didn't have a response to that. "I'd better get started. It was nice to see you again." Mitch said, then turned his back to her.

*

Aunt Bridget was cooking dinner for Mitch and herself when Sea came down from getting ready. Her aunt's face lit up when Sea walked into the kitchen.

"Wow! You look gorgeous, Sea. You clean up really well. Don't you think, Mitch?"

Mitch was sitting at the table playing computer games on his laptop when he glanced up to look at Sea. He was awestruck by her beauty. "Yeah, she looks nice." He didn't want to say what he was really thinking which was that she was the most beautiful woman he'd ever seen and was aroused from looking at her. When the women looked away, he adjusted himself.

"Nice?" Bridget exclaimed. "She's drop dead gorgeous!"

"Thanks, Aunt Bridget, but let's not put him on the spot. I already know how he feels."

"Why would you say that? Didn't you two just meet today?"

"Yes we did but earlier today, not when he came to the house. He is the one who helped me with my tire this morning."

"Really? Isn't that a coincidence! You must have been a little taken aback when you saw him at the door."

"I was. I thought he was stalking me at first."

"Mitch? No! Sweet as could be."

"I know that now." Sea said, as she looked at Mitch. He looked up and caught her eye.

"So what's going on here?" Sea asked. "You cook dinner for all your hired help?"

Bridget laughed. "Oh… no. I've known Mitch for a long time. His father is a good friend of mine." her aunt replied. "I like to pay him in home cooked meals, when I can. He doesn't get many of those anymore. I like his company too. He's a very smart man. I'm so thankful he knows about computers because I certainly don't. He comes over often to help me around the house or to update my computer for me. He's a handy person to have around."

"Too bad he doesn't know anything about cars." Sea said, as she giggled.

"Yeah, well, cars have never been my strong suit. I know plenty of other things though. I'm not completely useless," he said.

"I know. I'm only teasing."

Mitch was green with envy. Sea looked like an angel. He wanted to be the one going on the date with her. Not watching her smile and look excited about going out with someone else. That would have been him taking her out if he had had the guts to ask her out earlier that morning. He wanted to kick himself. He wondered if she would have accepted his offer. Mitch wasn't exactly a lady's man.

"It's fifteen minutes after eight o'clock. Your date is late." Mitch noted.

"I'm sure he'll be here any minute. He probably got caught in traffic."

After thirty more minutes, her date finally arrived.

"Hey, Mark. I'm glad you're here. I was starting to worry."

Mark kissed her on the cheek. "Hey, Sea. Sorry I'm late. I had to get gas first."

"No problem. I want you to meet my aunt." Sea gestured for him to enter the kitchen.

Mitch was waiting in anticipation. He wanted to know what type of guy Sea would go out with. He wasn't surprised once he saw him. He was the typical rugged good looking guy that every woman pined for. Mitch was no match for him.

"Mark, I want you to meet my Aunt Bridget. She's my father's sister. She has been kind enough to let me live with her awhile in this big house until I can find a place of my own. And, this is her friend,

Mitch."

Mark walked over to shake both their hands. "Hi, it's great to meet you, Bridget. When he walked over to shake Mitch's hand, Mark noticed that Mitch's handshake was more rigorous than a handshake should have been. "That's quite the handshake you got there, Mitch." Mark moved in closer to whisper to him. "If I didn't know better, I'd say you were jealous over my date. I mean she is a hot piece of ass after all." Mark swaggered away all smug and pleased with himself. Mitch sat there in disbelief and felt bad for Sea. She had no idea what she was walking into. He wanted to walk over and punch the guy but thought against it. He didn't want to ruin Sea's night.

When Mark walked over to shake Mitch's hand, Bridget whispered into Sea's ear. "He's very handsome, Sea. You certainly know how to pick 'em."

Sea smiled widely and said, "Thanks Aunt Bridget. I really like him." Bridget smiled back and said, "What's not to like?" They both giggled.

Sea grabbed her purse. "We better get going Mark. I'm pretty hungry and I'm excited to see what restaurant you're bringing me to."

"It was nice to meet you Bridget... Mitch." Mark said, as he winked at Mitch on the way out. As if to say, I have her and you don't. Mitch didn't trust him. He didn't want anything to happen to his friend's niece or the beautiful woman he just met this morning. He hardly knew her but felt that it was his duty to protect her from this creep.

"Bridget, I'm not feeling well. Would you mind making my dinner to go? I think I'll just go home and eat it. If... that's okay?"

"I'm sorry to hear that, Mitch. Sure. No problem." Bridget got everything together for him and soon he was on his way. Lucky for Mitch, Sea and Mark hadn't left yet. He thought it was odd since they seemed in a rush but all the better for him. Mitch crept around the bushes and quietly headed toward his car. He got in and waited for them to leave.

Sea was excited. She was disappointed she hadn't had time to go shopping for a new outfit but she was happy with what she had on. It was sexy enough. She found it odd that Mark didn't compliment her. Most men did, especially when she had her cleavage showing.

When they got to his car, Mark didn't open the door for her. He walked around to the driver side and jumped in. Sea was appalled. She expected a lot more from this guy. He was sweet and charming that morning. What happened? As she went to open the door, it stuck. He rolled down the window to give her instructions on how to open it. He told her to simply lift it up and then pull. It wasn't easy for her to do but she managed to get it open. It was a good thing he was good looking because his manners were lacking when other people weren't around. When she took a seat, she found it difficult to put her feet anywhere because of all the trash on the floor. She couldn't understand why anyone would leave their beautiful Ford Mustang looking so filthy. It had a rank odor as well. So far she was not impressed. Sea was becoming increasingly nervous about her precipitous date.

When Mark put his key in the ignition, his cellphone rang. "I'm sorry, Sea, I have to take this." He took his key out of the ignition and got out so he could have privacy. She opened her mouth in disbelief.

Sea couldn't believe this was happening to her. He wasn't presenting a very good first impression and now he was delaying their date even further. She was starving by this point. It was almost nine o'clock. She was having second thoughts because of his downright rudeness. Sea, being the insecure person that she was, tolerated a lot from men—especially guys that were good looking, because when she received attention from gorgeous men, that made her feel good about herself. She really wanted to give him a chance but her patience was running thin.

Mark finally finished up with his phone call, five minutes later. "Okay. Sorry again. My friend was having girlfriend problems. Let's go eat."

"I feel sorry for your friend." Sea said under her breath.

"What's that? I couldn't hear you."

"I said I'm hungry as a fiend."

When Mark finally pulled out of his parking space, Mitch followed about four car lengths behind. He tried not to be obvious. After about a mile, he saw their car swerve a bit every so often. He wondered what was going on in the car. After about another three miles of this, they pulled over onto the shoulder. Mitch did the same but turned his lights off so they wouldn't suspect anything. They sat there for quite a while. Mitch began to suspect that they were having sex. He wanted to think better of her but she had made her choice and now she was on her own. Everything seemed fine so he left. Mitch was disappointed. He had no respect for her anymore. He drove on past and went about two miles to find a place to turn around. On his way back, he didn't see the Mustang. It was gone. But, he saw something else. It was a woman walking down the street. It was Sea. Mitch slowed down and pulled off onto the shoulder.

He rolled down his window. "Are you okay? What happened to Mark?" he asked her.

"I'm fine. I don't want to talk about it. Can you take me home, please?"

"Sure. Hold on. Stay right there." Mitch jumped out to open the door for her.

"Thank you. What a gentleman. That's the second time today that you have saved me. I owe you one, no, make that two." Sea never thought she would be so happy to see him. "What are you doing out here? I thought you were having dinner with Bridget."

"Your aunt needed milk so I offered to go get her some. I left around the same time you did. I saw you walking on my way back from the store."

"Where's the milk?" Sea asked, thinking it was a bit strange since her aunt had shopped the day before.

"Oh... it's in the back. I didn't want it to fall off the front seat, if I stopped too quickly." Mitch felt bad for lying but he would have had a harder time telling the truth. He couldn't tell her that he was lurking in the shadows, like a creep.

"I like how clean your car is."

"Oh, thanks. I just cleaned it the other day. It was way overdue." Silence filled the air.

"I just want to go home and forget about this whole day." she said.

"Why? What happened with your date, if you don't mind me asking?"

Sea didn't answer.

Mitch wondered if Mark tried to hurt her or God forbid rape her. Why else would she get out of the car and try to get away from someone who looked like that?

"Did he hurt you?"

"No."

"Are you sure? I'll call the police, if you want me to."

"No, that's okay. He didn't do anything like that. He was being stupid and wouldn't listen to reason."

"What do you mean?"

"Mark's true colors came to light as soon as we left the house. I asked him to stop texting and driving but he refused and said that he was upset with me for not trusting him. He scared me to death when we went around a couple of turns because he kept swerving in and out of the dotted lines. I even caught him staring at himself in the mirror while driving. It was ridiculous. I had had enough. I begged him to pull over and let me out. He wasn't worth risking my life over. Let's just say that his good looks are all that he has going for him."

"Wow. He's a keeper." Mitch snickered. "I'm glad you figured this out early because he whispered something to me back at the house that was hard to keep from you."

"Really? What did he say?" Sea asked anxiously.

"He said that you were a hot piece of ass and winked at me as you two left. I wanted to punch him right then and there but didn't want to upset you or ruin your night, so I didn't."

"Thank you. I would've been upset. It's better that I figured it out for myself."

Mark was waiting for Sea when they arrived at her aunt's house.

Mitch shook his head. "Do you want me to ask him to leave? You don't have to talk to him."

"No. I'll be fine. This won't take long. He probably just came back to apologize. I don't think he'll do anything."

Mitch was not happy. He didn't want to leave her side. Sea walked over to talk to Mark as he leaned on his car. Mitch strained to hear their conversation as he walked toward the house. He didn't want to leave until Sea was safely inside.

"What do you want, Mark?" Sea asked, disgusted with him.

"I wanted to make sure you made it home safely. I felt bad about leaving you there on the side of the road. I went back to see if you were still there. I became worried when I couldn't find you."

"Why? I told you to. I can take care of myself. You need to leave."

"I was rude and I'm sorry. Can we start over? Give me another chance."

"You are beyond rude. You are way too into yourself for me to date. I have no interest in you anymore, so please leave."

Sea stepped back to walk away but Mark grabbed her by the wrist to stop her.

"Wait!" Mark said angrily.

"Let go of me!" Sea called out.

Mitch saw and came running across the lawn to help.

"Get your hand off of her. You heard her. You need to leave."

Mitch took Mark's hand off of Sea. Mark pushed him when he did.

Sea put her hand on Mitch's chest to keep him from retaliating. She stood between them trying to prevent a fight.

"What's your problem, Sea? What? You prefer this loser over me? He plays computer games. He's a faggot. You need someone like me. I promise I won't text and drive again. Give me another chance." Mark was getting really agitated and demanded that she listen. Sea became afraid. She wanted Mark to leave but she didn't know how to make him listen to reason.

"Can't you see that he is obsessed with you? How did the geek know where you were? Did you stop to think how he was able to find you so quickly? He was out there already. He followed us. He's a creep."

"Is that true, Mitch? You followed us? You said you went out to get milk. Let me see the milk, Mitch." Sea walked over to his car and opened up the back door. She didn't find any milk. "You lied to me Mitch. There's no milk."

Mitch turned beet red. He couldn't believe this was happening to him. He had only tried to protect her.

"I know. I'm sorry I lied. I couldn't tell you the truth. You wouldn't have understood. I thought you were in danger after he said what he did. I was trying to protect you. I was right! You said it yourself, he's a scumbag."

"You know what? Both of you leave!"

"Sea? You don't mean that." Mitch said in shock.

"Yes, I do."

Mitch had a stupefied expression on his face.

Mark started laughing at him. "What a loser," he said, as he shook his head.

"Excuse me. You think you're better than him," Sea said in disgust.

"Yes. I'm far better than him." Mark's overconfidence was oozing out by then.

"I have no idea how you could possibly think that after tonight. Since the moment you picked me up, you have been a complete ass," Sea said in exasperation. "You show up late. You didn't bother to open your broken car door for me or clean your filthy car before you picked me up. You made me wait even further when you answered your cellphone. And, texting and driving is against the law and you endangered my life by being so careless. You are definitely not better than Mitch."

Mark gave her a look of haughty disdain and walked away. "Whatever. I don't need this. I'm out of here." Mark shoved passed Mitch on the way back to his car and drove away.

Mitch slowly walked back to his car. He turned and said, "I'm sorry I lied to you. I thought there was a chance he might hurt you. I only wanted to protect you. I really did have your best interests at heart."

Sea could tell that Mitch was being genuine. "Thanks, Mitch. I appreciate that, but I can take care of myself."

"Of course you can."

Mitch didn't want to leave but he knew he had to. He opened his car door and climbed in. He suddenly felt very depressed. Having disappointed Sea tugged at his heart. His goal was to impress her, not repel her. Mitch started hitting the steering wheel and cursing out loud for screwing up.

Knock! Knock! Knock! Mitch jumped.

"Let me in!" It was Sea trying to get his attention.

Mitch rolled down the passenger side window. "What's going on?" he asked.

"Unlock the door. I want to talk to you. Please."

Mitch unlocked the door. She sat down next to him and closed the door.

"I know you meant well, but you can't go around stalking people. It's creepy."

"I know. You and Mark made that perfectly clear. That's what you wanted to say to me?"

"There's more. I just wanted to make sure we were clear on that point. My Aunt Bridget obviously cares a lot about you. I trust her judgment. I truly believe you're a good person. I knew Mark wouldn't leave unless I asked you to leave as well. Also, I was upset you lied to me."

She waited for a response.

"I couldn't tell you the truth. I was too afraid of what you might think of me. I really am sorry."

"I know you are." Sea smiled at him and said, "Can we be friends?" She offered her hand for him to shake.

"Sure. Friends." Mitch shook her hand back.

Mitch chuckled.

Sea frowned. "What? Did I do something funny?"

"No." Mitch gave her a great big smile and said, "I want to ask you something."

"What?" Sea was curious now.

Mitch hesitated. His palms were sweaty and his heart was racing.

"What is it?" Sea was starting to get impatient. She was exhausted and wanted to go to bed.

Mitch finally blurted out, "Do you want to go bowling with me on Saturday?" Mitch couldn't believe he got the words out. His heart was racing.

Sea stared at him for a minute. She didn't know what to think. "As a date?"

Mitch wanted to start off slow. "No. I want to go as friends. My dad and I go bowling every Saturday. Sometimes Bridget will go too. We should all go together. That way, you and I can get to know one another better. We will be bumping into each other over here quite often. You can't get rid of me that easily."

They both laughed.

"I'm glad I met you today Sea."

"Me too. It's definitely been one long day. It's not often a girl gets rescued twice in one day. Thanks for watching out for me, Mitch. I owe you now. I'll pay for the first game and a round of beer."

"That sounds good. I'm looking forward to it."

"Me too. Have a good night."

CHAPTER EIGHT

"Can I get four beers please?" Sea asked the bartender.

Sea grabbed the beers and headed toward lane five. "Someone take these before I drop one," Sea called.

Mitch jumped up from his chair and grabbed two beers out of her hand to lighten her load.

"Thanks." Sea said, as she sat down. "Where's your father? Isn't he coming?"

"Yes. He should be here soon."

A few minutes later, a tall man started making his way toward their lane. Sea wondered if that could be his father.

"Hey Dad!" Mitch stood up to give his dad a hug. "Dad, this is Bridget's niece, Sea. Sea, this is my dad, Michael."

Michael walked over to where she was sitting. "It's nice to meet you Sea. That's an interesting name. How do you spell it?"

"S-E-A." Sea spelled out. "My dad liked to draw pictures of the sea when he was younger."

"That's great. I like it." Michael said.

Mitch picked up a beer and handed it to his dad.

"What's this?" Michael asked.

"Sea bought the first round already. This one is yours," Mitch answered.

Bridget finished entering their names. "You're up first, Sea."

"Okay. I'm pretty rusty at this. It's been almost ten years since I've bowled."

"That's okay. Bridget isn't that great either." Michael said, as he looked at Bridget and winked.

"That's very funny, Michael. I'm not that bad. I had about eighty-five points the last time we bowled."

"This is true," Michael said, as he chuckled. "Let's see if you can beat that score."

"If I do, what will you give me?" Bridget playfully asked.

"I'll take you out to dinner next weekend."

"I better bowl my heart out then," she said, as she fixed Michael's crooked collar.

"Let's make this interesting. How about Dad and Bridget on one team, me and Sea on the other. How does that sound?"

"Sounds good to me," Michael said.

"Okay." Sea said, as she held the ten-pound ball. Her first roll was a gutter ball. When she walked back to grab another ball, she saw a pained look on everyone's face. She laughed it off and tried again. On her second roll, she knocked three pins down. Mitch clapped for her and said, "It's okay. You'll do better next time." Sea sat down and sipped her beer.

Next, it was Michael's turn. He walked up to the lane, held the ball with both hands for a few seconds, then fiercely swung it down the lane so it would curve toward the center of the pins. His first roll was a strike. Bridget stood up and gave Michael two high fives.

"Bridget seems to be enjoying herself," Sea observed.

"Yeah. Your aunt can be quite competitive sometimes. She's been so busy with her artwork lately that she hasn't been able to bowl with Dad and me for a while now. I like watching her have fun. She doesn't do it often enough. Thanks to you, she now has time to do other things. I'm really glad you're here to help her. She does too much."

"It's your turn, Mitch," Bridget called.

Mitch walked up and knocked down eight pins. On his second roll, he nailed the last two and got a spare.

Finally, it was Bridget's turn. She was excited to get as many pins down as possible. She wanted that dinner date. Everyone watched her carry her ball to the lane and stop. She remained still for about five seconds. You could tell that she was concentrating hard. On her first roll, she knocked down five pins. Everyone clapped for her. She was antsy waiting for her ball to return. Her second roll was a gutter ball. She swung too far to the left trying to hit two pins on the side but missed. She had a disappointed look on her face when she sat down.

The round completed. Sea was up again. On her second attempt, she knocked six pins down on her first roll and nailed three pins on her second. She was delighted to hit the pins and get a decent score that time.

"Did you grow up around here?" Sea asked Mitch, as she sat back down.

"Yes. I've lived here my whole life. My mother and your aunt went to high school together and were best friends. Bridget was my mom's maid of honor. After my mom had me, Bridget would babysit whenever my mom needed her to."

"Where's your mother now?" Sea asked.

"She passed away when I was a little kid," he answered. "After my mother died, Bridget took me under her wing and became like a second mother to me. That's why she likes to fix me home-cooked meals and makes excuses to have me over all the time. It's fine by me though, I like spending time with her. She's easy to talk to."

"Yes. She is. I'm very fond of her. I always enjoyed visiting with her when my family journeyed north. She accepts me just the way I am. My mother is another story. She prefers I go to school and pursue a respectable career."

"Is your mom a doctor?"

"Yes. She's a psychiatrist."

"Well, what do you want to do?"

"I don't know yet. I'm still figuring that part out. I know I don't want to be like my mother. She spent more time with her patients than she did with us. She's never been fond of children. Work is her comfort zone."

"Oh. I forgot to tell you. I got the job," she said. "The manager called me early this morning to tell me."

"On a Saturday?"

"Yeah. He wanted to make sure I started on Monday. He was too busy to call on Friday."

"Oh. That's great, Sea. Congratulations. Are you nervous?"

"No. Not really. I'm excited to get a paycheck. I'm running low on my reserves. The work I'm doing for Bridget should help out some before I get my first paycheck."

"We're trying to bowl here. Stop your yammering and take your turn, Mitch," Bridget called out.

"So serious, Bridget. You'd think you were expecting to win or something."

"I am. And we will." Bridget said playfully.

Mitch threw the ball and got a strike. Sea jumped up and cheered for her teammate as she made her way up to take her turn. She grabbed her ball.

"What are you doing, Sea? It's my turn." her aunt called out to her.

"Oh. Sorry. My bad." Sea put the ball back and sat down.

On her third attempt, Sea collected seven pins.

"So what brings you to Northampton?" Mitch asked, when they finally sat back down.

"I wanted a fresh start. My fiancé broke off our engagement a few months before the wedding." Sea answered.

"Do you mind if I ask why?"

"For now, yes. I'm not ready to tell you everything—or anyone for that matter. It's a long story and I'm not ready to face it myself yet."

"Of course, I understand." Mitch said. He didn't know what to make of it, and hoped that it wasn't unfaithfulness on her part. His curiosity was definitely sparked and he wanted to know more.

Sea got up to bowl her fifth round. At the end of the fifth, Sea had thirty points and Mitch had sixty-five.

"So what do you do for a living, Mitch?" Sea asked.

"I'm a computer programmer at Lartek Industries." Mitch replied.

"How long have you been doing that?"

"For about three years now. The economy was so bad after I graduated from college that it took me two years to finally find this job. I had to work as a waiter to make ends meet. I heard about a position opening up while working at the restaurant. I became friends with some of the regulars and heard one of them talking about the company needing a good computer programmer. I jumped at the chance."

"Wow, that's really great. Good for you." Sea said enthusiastically.

"So, do you have any siblings?" Mitch asked.

"Yes. I have an older sister. Her name is Sarah. She's been married for over six years and has two young boys." she said. "Do you have any brothers or sisters?"

"No. I'm an only child. It's just me and my dad.

"Where does your family live?"

"They live near my sister in Annapolis, Maryland."

"Your dad and Bridget seem pretty close. Are they…?"

"No. I don't think so. As far as I know, they are just good friends."

"Would you mind if they were more than friends?" Sea asked.

"I don't think so. I love Bridget like a mother already. She's been very good for my dad. They talk often on the phone. I think he gets very lonely at times, and she does, too. I'd give them my blessing, if they asked me." he replied.

"It would be so cute if they were together." she said. "I like Michael. They would make a great couple. Maybe we should try to set them up."

"I don't think that's a good idea. I believe Bridget wants to live by herself. She spends so much time working on her art that she wouldn't have time to devote to a husband. It wouldn't be fair to my dad. I don't think they would appreciate it if you tried to play matchmaker."

"Maybe you're right. If they did get married, you and I would be related."

Mitch wasn't sure what she meant by that. Did Sea like him or did she not want to be related to him? "Are you saying that would be a bad thing?"

"Ummm, oh look, it's my turn." Sea didn't realize she had said something so revealing until it was too late. She was glad for the distraction. She didn't know how she felt about Mitch yet. He was nice but he was certainly not her type. He wasn't ugly but he wasn't great looking either. She never really cared for men who were balding. But there was something about him she couldn't walk away from. He had a gentle nature and was very thoughtful. Mitch had qualities that her past boyfriends lacked. Was she ready to try something new? Would she be truly happy if he wasn't great looking?

Sea walked up to Mitch after he bowled his turn and asked him, "How would you feel if we were related? Would it bother you?"

"No. I wouldn't be bothered. It would be nice to have a cousin.

I don't have any yet."

"But I thought you liked me."

"I do like you but it would be great to be connected to you in a different way too. We could still get married if we wanted to. We wouldn't be blood related." As Mitch said those words, Sea blushed and felt uncomfortable. Feelings were out in the open and it didn't seem to bother Mitch. His reaction surprised her. When they first met, he was nervous and shy around her.

"Your frankness and honesty are refreshing Mitch. I like this new you."

"There's no point in denying it, when you clearly know how I feel."

"This is true." she said.

Michael and Bridget won the match. Michael bowled a total of six strikes and Bridget got her highest score ever.

Despite the loss, Sea and Mitch had a great time.

"I had fun, Mitch. Thanks for inviting me."

"We should hang out again sometime."

"Is next weekend too soon?" Sea asked.

"No. That sounds good. I'm surprised you want to hang out again so soon."

"I like hanging out with you. You're easy to talk to. Plus, I still owe you for rescuing me from the side of the road."

"You don't owe me anything for that. You needed help and I was there."

"I know but I want to reward you for your chivalry."

"Okay. I know a great place we can go for dinner. Shall we bring

Bridget and Dad with us?"

"No. It should be just the two of us this time." she said.

Mitch was happy with that answer.

CHAPTER NINE

Mitch brought Sea to a nice café around the corner from his apartment.

"Do you like the food?" he asked.

"Yes. The food here is great. I wasn't sure what to think of it at first. The place doesn't look like much from the outside."

"I know. I thought the same thing too at first, but ever since my dad took me here I've come often for lunch and dinner." Mitch said. "Sometimes I take Bridget here to get her out of the house."

"Oh. That's nice of you. Thanks for taking such good care of my aunt. I'm sure she really appreciates it."

"I'm stuffed." Sea said, as she put her hand on her belly. "I'm glad we came here. We should try this place again sometime."

Mitch grinned.

"What makes you think I'm going to go out with you again?" he teased.

"Because you like spending time with me—don't you?" she said, as she cocked her head to the side in disbelief.

"Oh. Really?"

"Yes. Really." They both laughed.

Sea paid the check. As they were leaving the café, Sea's high heel got caught in one of the drain grates right outside the door. As she struggled to free herself, her heel broke off. When it did, Sea couldn't maintain her balance. Before she fell to the ground, Mitch caught her.

"Are you okay?" he asked.

"Yeah. I'm okay. I think I twisted my ankle though." she answered.

Sea tried to walk on it but didn't get far. Mitch could tell that she wouldn't be able to walk back to his apartment unassisted.

Mitch scooped her up and started walking back to his apartment. Sea was impressed by his strength. She rested her head on his shoulder and felt comfortable in his arms. He was thankful his apartment was close by. Once they arrived at his apartment complex, he carried her up three flights of stairs. He was exhausted by the time they reached his door.

"Are you okay?" she asked. "I feel bad."

"Yeah, I'll live." He thought it was worth it.

Once the front door was open, he picked her up and placed her on the couch. When he set her down, Sea looked up into his eyes and said, "I never noticed this before but you have gorgeous green eyes."

"Mitch felt a tingle go up his spine. He wanted to kiss her in that moment but it was too soon. He didn't want to scare her off.

"Thanks for carrying me Mitch. Not many guys would have done that."

"I don't want this night to end." he said.

"I don't want this night to end either…"

"Let me see if I can find an ace bandage for you."

From where Sea sat, she could see hundreds of DVDs and a big television screen, which screamed bachelor pad. Star Trek and Star Wars memorabilia decorated the room. She didn't hate it but she wasn't impressed either.

It didn't take long for Mitch to find the ace bandage.

"Here you go." Mitch handed Sea an aspirin and a glass of water.

Sea took it with a smile.

As she swallowed the aspirin, Mitch rolled up her jeans a little way so he could properly place the ace bandage around her ankle.

"You're really sweet for doing this, Mitch."

"Do you want to watch a movie?" Mitch asked. He was getting anxious and didn't know what to do next.

"No. Let's sit and talk. So… what's up with all the spaceships? It's not very girl-friendly."

"I know. I'm planning to put it up on eBay. Hopefully I can make some extra cash from it. It's time to move on. I'm almost thirty." Mitch had wanted to clear it out before she came over. He wasn't counting on her seeing his place so soon.

"Would you like help redecorating your place, once you clear out some stuff?" she offered.

"That would be great. It could definitely use a woman's touch."

Sea paused for a few moments and then asked, "How old were you when your mother died?"

"I was eight."

"How did she die, if you don't mind me asking?"

"She died in a car accident, hit and run."

"I'm so sorry." Sea said.

"It was a long time ago."

"You told me a little about your mom, what is your dad like? he asked.

"He's a great man. He's strong, kind, funny, forgiving, emotionally available—unlike my mother—and very loving."

"What does he do for a living?"

"He paints the inside and outside of houses."

"Sounds like you were raised by your dad if your mom wasn't in the picture much."

"I was. I hardly ever saw my mother. She worked all day. I'm very close with my dad. My mom is like a stranger to me. I'm not sure what my dad sees in her. They have a strange relationship. My sister, Sarah, was a trooper. My parents expected a lot from her since she was older. I looked up to her. She was like a mother to me in many ways. She would come and comfort me whenever I was upset. My mother was too preoccupied with her career to properly raise us. She thinks the only things in life that matter, are money and prestige."

"I'm sorry to hear that. Your dad and sister did a fine job though," Mitch said with a smile.

"I love them both very much. I miss them. I was close to my sister for most of my life, until recently. She didn't want me to move but I left anyway. Too many bad memories. I haven't talked to her since I moved up here. It's a long story. Someday, I'll tell you about it."

"What's your favorite color?" Mitch asked.

Sea chuckled. "Ummm… I'd have to say blue like the sea. Why?"

"I was curious and some day that information might come in handy. Plus, I wanted to change the subject. It was getting too serious in here."

"What's your favorite color?"

"Black."

Sea chuckled again. "Black? Why black?"

"I'm obsessed with Darth Vader and he wears all black." Mitch smiled. He looked at her to see if she could tell that he was joking.

"I'm kidding. I like black because it reminds me of my mother. My best memories of her are at bedtime. She used to tell me stories of when she was a little girl—how her father would point out the constellations to her and she would spend hours looking up at the stars. It's strange, I know, but black is somehow comforting to me."

"That's not strange. I think it's great. You're lucky to have had a mother who loved you as much as she did and took time out of her day to spend with you. I envy that."

"It's not too late for you. Your mom is still alive. You could try to reach out to her somehow."

"I don't know. She's hard to be around. We don't have many conversations without fighting. She's stubborn in her own way and I'm stubborn in mine."

"Is there anything you both have in common? Maybe that's the way in."

"I never thought about it before," she said. "You're right though. I should appreciate what I have. I'll have to think on it."

"What about your father? When's the last time you talked to

him?" he asked.

"It's been a while. I think I'll call him soon though. I really miss him. A week after I turned thirteen, I had come down with the flu. He left work early to come pick me up from school. He checked up on me during his lunch breaks that week. He's such a great dad."

"What's your favorite movie?" Sea asked.

" 'Braveheart.' What's yours?"

" 'Misery.' I love a good Stephen King thriller."

"I'm getting sleepy." she yawned. "I want to keep talking but I'm afraid I might fall asleep right here if I do."

"That's okay. I'm getting pretty tired myself. I know it's unorthodox since we still don't know each other that well but would you mind sleeping here tonight? I'm exhausted and I don't think I have the strength to carry you to the car."

"I don't know..." Sea hesitated.

"I promise to be a gentleman." Mitch assured her. "I can put clean sheets on my bed for you and I'll sleep on the couch. My bedroom door locks if you're concerned. I have a spare toothbrush in the closet and you can borrow one of my t-shirts for pajamas."

"Are you sure? I don't want to put you out. I don't need to lock the door, I trust you." Sea gave Mitch a sweet smile.

"I'll go make the bed."

"I'll call my aunt to let her know I'm here and won't be coming home tonight, so she won't worry."

"Sounds like a plan," Mitch said from down the hall.

*

Sea awoke to the smell of coffee and bacon. As she rolled over and stretched, she could hear Mitch in the kitchen, whistling. She laid her head back down on the pillow and thought about everything that had happened the night before. She wanted to savor the memory of that moment. Mitch wasn't the type of guy she usually dated, but she was happy and felt safe with him. It was romantic the way he carried her up three flights of stairs and wrapped her foot. And now, he was fixing breakfast for her. Trevor never cooked. He would take her out to eat a lot but he never wanted to cook, even if she offered to help. Trevor made good money and was polite, but sometimes he was selfish and domineering. Maybe Trevor did her a favor by breaking off the engagement. If he truly loved her, he would have stayed. She didn't want to be with someone like that. She wanted to be with someone like Mitch. He was caring, kind, honest and selfless. Sure he lied about the milk but it was a white lie. Mitch was average-looking compared to her other boyfriends, but she was starting to see past all that. He was beautiful on the inside.

Sea got dressed and limped out to the kitchen.

"Wow. It smells good out here. What are we having for breakfast?"

"I'm making scrambled eggs, bacon, toast, hash browns and cutting up fruit. I don't usually eat fruit but I thought you would like it. I hope you're hungry."

Sea was pleased by what she saw and smelled. "I'm famished. I overslept this morning. I slept like a rock last night. Your bed is really comfortable. Thanks for letting me have it."

"You're welcome." Mitch was grinning from ear to ear. "How's your ankle?"

"It's much better, thanks. I can actually walk on it now."

Mitch and Sea enjoyed their breakfast together. Afterward, he drove her home. When he pulled up to her aunt's house, Sea leaned over and gave Mitch a hug.

"I had a great time, Mitch. Let's do this again soon."

Mitch was eager to see her again. "Is tomorrow too soon? I could bring a movie over for us to watch while you rest your ankle."

Sea nodded her head. "That would be great."

CHAPTER TEN

Two weeks later, Mitch drove Sea to Highland Lake for the afternoon. He enjoyed listening to Sea sing along with the radio. He thought she had a pretty voice. He chuckled to himself when she would sing the wrong words to the song.

"Have you been to this lake before?" Sea asked.

"Yes. When I was a kid, my parents brought me here every summer." Mitch answered. "My mom loved to take pictures of the beautiful scenery. She would also tell Dad and me to sit here or stand there but we decided to make funny faces instead. She would laugh and take our pictures anyway."

"I have a surprise for you." Mitch said, when they pulled into the parking lot.

"Oh yeah? What?" Sea said enthusiastically.

Mitch jumped out of the car and opened the trunk. Sea could see him pulling out a basket and blanket.

"We're having a picnic?" Sea said excitedly as she got out of the car.

"You sound surprised."

"I am. I haven't been on a picnic since I was little. What made you think to have a picnic?"

"I thought we'd get hungry later. Only makes sense." Mitch teased.

"No." Sea laughed. "I mean what made you think of this?"

They found a nice shady spot. Sea helped Mitch unfold the blanket and spread it on the ground. They sat opposite one another. Mitch took items out of the basket one by one.

"Bridget suggested it. She had heard on the news that it was supposed to be a bright sunny day today and thought a picnic would be the perfect outing for us. She bought all the items and made the sandwiches for me. I think she liked the idea of us hanging out together."

"Why do you say that?"

"I guess she's worried about me. Not that long ago, she asked me why I haven't settled down yet. I told her that I haven't found the right girl yet. I came close once, but it didn't work out. I've dated a few girls since then, but they were not what I was looking for. I don't want to settle for just anyone. I want to be with someone I can spend the rest of my life with."

"What happened with the girl you almost married?"

"Well, four years ago I was engaged to a girl I met in college. She loved to play the violin. It was her passion. We dated for three years and we were so much in love. A month after I proposed, she received an offer to play in The New York Philharmonic Orchestra. She couldn't pass it up and I didn't want her to. I told her I would quit my job and go with her but she decided against it. She wanted to focus on her music instead. She told me she would have to practice her music for long hours and that I would be a distraction.

"Why was she dating anyone if she wanted to focus on her music?"

"When I met her, she was teaching violin lessons to youngsters. She auditioned for several places but most said no, so she assumed no one would want her. After those rejections, she acknowledged that being a professional violinist was not in her future. She decided to focus on having a family instead. I naively supported that decision. I should've known better but I was blinded by love. She simply loved her music more than me."

"I'm sorry she hurt you. It could've happened to anyone though."

"Yeah. I suppose. Thanks." Mitch said. "I'm glad she received the letter before we were married. It would've been a whole lot messier if she hadn't."

"Yes. I think you're right. Was she the only one?"

"Only one I've loved? Yes. I dated this one girl I began to fall for, but after four months I found out that she was cheating on me. She moved in two weeks prior. If you're going to cheat, it's probably not a good idea to leave your phone lying around where your significant other could find it. Her boy toy on the side texted her while she was in the shower and I saw it. By the time she got out of the shower, I had half her stuff packed. She left an hour later and I never saw her again."

"Wow." Sea said. "I haven't been cheated on but some guys seem to want only one thing when they date me. There aren't a lot of serious guys out there. Or, maybe, I'm just not good at finding them. Who knows?"

"Have you ever..." Mitch began to ask.

"Have I what? Have I ever cheated?" Sea hesitated before she answered. "Yes. Once. I'm not proud of it and I deeply regretted it. Why did you ask me that?"

"I thought maybe that was why your fiancé broke up with you."

"No. He's not the one I cheated on. It was someone before him. Why would you assume that?"

"I guess I don't have a very good imagination. I couldn't really think of any other reasons why your fiancé broke up with you. And, sorry for saying this, but it was a bit shallow of you to date someone because of how they looked and not what's on the inside."

"Wow. That was hurtful Mitch."

"I wasn't trying to hurt you but you inadvertently hurt me too."

"How?" Sea said surprised.

"You accepted a date with Mark two minutes after you met him simply because of how he looked. With me, you'd rather be friends because of how I look."

"I don't know what to say. I'm speechless."

They ate in silence for a while. It seemed like an eternity for Mitch. He felt uneasy about what he had said, but wanted to be truthful with her. No secrets. Mitch didn't eat very much; neither did Sea.

"You're not totally innocent here." Sea piped up.

"What do you mean?"

"If you think this way about me and still want to be friends, then you're guilty of it too. You're putting up with it because I'm pretty. Aren't you?"

Mitch laughed. "Touché."

"I like how frank you are Mitch. It's a little infuriating but I like it. You know, if we do become a couple, I can't guarantee that it will be perfect. That's a lot of pressure."

"I don't expect you to be perfect but honest about how you feel and what you want."

"It's not easy for me to open up about certain things but, I will try." Sea said, as she ate her cheese and sipped her wine. "Thanks for taking me here Mitch. This place is awesome. The sun is shining, the birds are chirping and I love the wind blowing in my hair. This lunch is great too, Aunt Bridget outdid herself."

"I agree. It's delicious."

Out of the blue, Sea placed his right hand above her left breast so he could feel her heart racing.

"Why is your heart beating so fast?" Mitch asked. "Do I make you nervous?"

"Yes."

"Why?"

"Because you see—me—warts and all. Other guys didn't care about the real me because they were too selfish and narcissistic to notice. They saw my looks and what I could do for them—to make them look good. That's why my fiancé broke up with me, because I wasn't able to give him what he wanted anymore. His selfish family didn't approve of me either. If I didn't appear perfect, he didn't want me. I never realized how selfish he was until now.

"You seem perfect to me." Mitch commented.

Sea smiled. She began to stare at him.

"What?"

She continued to stare. "I like your eyes. They're so green—like fresh grass."

Mitch chuckled. "That's a new one. I've never heard that before. Thanks… I guess."

Sea leaned in and gave Mitch a kiss on the cheek. She waited for a reaction. He looked surprised. After a moment, she came toward him again, tilted her head to the side and gave him a soft kiss on the lips. As she slowly backed away from him, Mitch wrapped his hands around her face to pull her in again. He wanted more. Sea didn't object. She parted her lips so they could kiss deeper. Her whole body was tingling and she melted in his arms. She was in ecstasy. Mitch laid her down on the blanket so they could be more comfortable. It was the first time that Sea had experienced a kiss as passionate as that one. Mitch poured out everything he had inside himself and gave it all to her in that kiss.

"Wow… wow…" Sea couldn't utter much more.

Mitch smiled broadly and held her in his arms.

"You want some more wine?" Mitch lifted the wine bottle and gestured it toward her.

Sea shook her head no. "I'd love some water. It's getting hot out here." Mitch handed her a bottle of water. She took a big gulp, then another.

"You want to go for a walk?" he asked.

"Sure." she said.

Mitch helped her up from the blanket.

"I have to say—that was a great kiss Mitch."

Mitch smiled. "I try."

Sea laughed and then hugged him.

They went for a long walk in the park with their arms wrapped around each other.

CHAPTER ELEVEN

The bike trails in Northampton were really spectacular in the fall. The foliage had started decaying, but the reds, oranges and yellows made the leaves seem more alive. With the cool breeze whipping through their hair, Sea and Mitch walked the path for about two miles. They talked about their childhoods, aspirations, likes and dislikes, fears and what they had learned from past relationships. As they talked, they took in the gorgeous scenery around them. On their walk back, they admired the beautiful sunset on the horizon, the sky filled with streaks of orange and pink.

Mitch savored every moment he spent with Sea. He couldn't believe that this beautiful woman wanted to be with him. For the last two months, he felt like he was in a dream and didn't want to wake up. He was nervous about them having sex. Would he measure up? Did she want to have sex with him? He was willing to be patient and wait for her, but for how long? Was she hiding something from him?

Sea was falling hard for Mitch. He was everything her other boyfriends hadn't been—he was genuine, attentive and caring. Sea was soaking it all in. He made her feel like she mattered. After two months, she still had butterflies in her stomach whenever she was around him. She could tell how much Mitch liked her or maybe even loved her now. She felt badly that they hadn't slept together yet. He was so patient that she wanted to be with him even more. She was nervous about him seeing her scars. The scars would bring questions that she wasn't ready to answer. She could see herself settling down with him but she couldn't face his disappointment upon learning that she couldn't have kids. Would he still want her if he found out? Sea was too afraid to ask.

*

"So… where is this mysterious woman you've been talking about? Or is she a figment of your imagination?" his best friend teased.

Mitch gave Tommy an annoyed look and punched him in the shoulder.

"Oww! What was that for?" Tommy said, as he rubbed his shoulder. "I was just playing. I'm sure she's great… since she lives in your head." Mitch punched him harder this time and then they started rough housing.

"Why can't you face the fact that she's not real?" Tommy said, as Mitch had him in a headlock.

"She is too, and she'll be here any minute so you better behave." Mitch said, as he finally let Tommy go.

"Fine," Tommy said, as he stood up.

They quieted down quickly when they heard a knock at the door.

"She's here." Tommy jumped up from the couch seconds before Mitch did. Tommy opened the door. His mouth dropped open. He couldn't believe that this hot chick would have anything to do with his best friend that he had known since childhood. His friend had never dated anyone this fine before. He figured there must be something wrong with her. Tommy thought Mitch was a great guy but he wasn't exactly a chick magnet. Mitch hadn't had sex with a girl until he was twenty.

"Hello there," Tommy said, trying to act suave and sophisticated. "Come in. It's nice to finally meet you. Mitch talks about you all the time but I didn't think you actually existed—until now."

Sea smiled politely and entered Tommy's apartment.

"Would you like a beer?" Tommy offered.

"It's eleven in the morning. I think I'll pass." Sea gave Mitch a questioning look.

Tommy popped off the cap of a beer bottle and started drinking. He gave them both a satisfied look when he finished. "Burrrp! Excuse me."

Sea looked away in disgust. She tried to make polite conversation for Mitch's sake. "So… what do you do for a living Tommy?"

"I'm a male stripper," Tommy said, looking at Sea with a straight face.

She laughed. He was full of it. He was clearly overweight and not sexy in the least.

"What? You don't believe me. I can be sexy." Tommy took off his shirt and started playing with his nipples while he wiggled his hips.

Sea laughed uncontrollably.

Mitch had hoped his friend would behave, but he should have known better.

"No… seriously… what do you do?" Sea asked again, still laughing.

"I'm an assistant manager at a movie theatre."

"Do you watch all the movies that come in?"

"Most of them, but some I'm not really interested in."

"How long have you known each other?"

"Since birth, practically." Tommy said. "Mitch and I were born only a few months apart, and every time our mothers visited, Mitch and I would play together or rough house. My mom went through a real depression when Mitch's mom died. They were very close—like sisters."

"I'm sorry to hear that. If Mitch's mom was anything like he is, she must have been pretty special."

"She was." Tommy said.

"I thought your mom was best friends with my aunt." Sea looked at Mitch.

"Well, it was the three of them, Bridget, Maggie and Claire, but Bridget was left out a bit when our mothers had us. Bridget would still see them, but Maggie and Claire were closer. Bridget wanted to focus on her artwork instead of having a family. Ceramics were her passion. Bridget was never the domestic type. She loved her freedom too much. They all hung out together in high school though. Tommy's mom, Claire, was the trouble-maker as you can easily guess, and my mom was more studious, but they all got along. Claire and Bridget would fight at times but my mother, Maggie, was the glue that kept everyone together. She always made sure they made up in the end."

"You guys hungry? I'm starving. Let's go eat." Tommy announced.

"Didn't you just eat a few hours ago?" Mitch asked.

"Yes, but I'm hungry again." Tommy quickly answered back.

"I could eat. I didn't have any breakfast today." Sea said.

*

Tommy, Mitch and Sea spent most of the afternoon playing pool and throwing darts at the local pub where they ate lunch. In the late afternoon, Sea started drinking cosmopolitans, continuing on through dinner. She became very tipsy. She was slurring her words and giggling every time she would hiccup. Tommy was having a blast but Mitch was becoming anxious and annoyed by her behavior.

"Let's go Sea. It's time to go home and sleep it off," Mitch said, as he was gathering her things.

"Don'th... be... satch... a... parrie... pooer. I... haffing... fuh." Sea could hardly get the words out and was making it difficult for them to leave the pub as she kept trying to talk to everyone there.

Mitch didn't have a choice. He scooped her up and carried her to his car. When he finally got her in the car, she fell asleep. Tommy was wobbling his way behind them back to the car, laughing and singing the whole way. After Mitch dropped Tommy off, he brought Sea back to his place.

Slap! Slap! Slap! "Wake up Sea!" Mitch shook Sea several times to try to wake her. He didn't want to carry her up three flights of stairs this time. He was too annoyed. She was so intoxicated it took him ten minutes to wake her up. When she finally did, Mitch slowly helped her climb the stairs. It took all his strength to keep her from falling down the stairs, so it took a while for him to get her into his apartment. He removed her jacket and shoes and then laid her down. Afterward, Mitch went out to the living room and plopped down on the couch. He didn't sleep much that night.

*

Sea awoke with a horrible hangover. Her mouth was dry and it felt like a cotton ball had taken up residency. She moaned and groaned when Mitch pulled back the drapes to let the light in.

"Don't! That's too bright. Close it!" Sea pulled the blanket over her head.

"It's time to get up Sea. I have to bring you home. I have errands to run today and half the day is gone. It's already one o'clock."

Sea got up as fast as her headache would allow and walked swiftly to the bathroom to vomit in the toilet. After she was done, she went right back to bed. "I'm never going to drink again. My head is spinning in a thousand directions." Sea placed her arm over her eyes to keep the light out.

Mitch went to the kitchen to make her a drink that would alleviate her hangover. "Here. Drink this. It will make you feel better."

Sea complied.

"Why did you drink so much last night?" Mitch asked.

Sea was hoping that Mitch would let last night go but, now—she could see that he wasn't. When Tommy was talking about Mitch and himself when they were kids, Sea ached for the same down the road. Before the shooting, she had planned to share that with her sister—to raise their babies together. Yesterday was a wakeup call. She was living in a fantasy world with Mitch, thinking she could make him happy. How could she ever make him happy if she couldn't have children? She thought Mitch would make a great dad some day. For the rest of the night, Sea couldn't get the thought out of her head. She felt guilty and ashamed.

Sea slowly answered. "I'm afraid of how I feel. I've never met anyone like you before. You make me so happy but I feel like I can't give you what you need. You deserve better than me."

"What are you talking about?" Mitch was getting agitated.

"I love you." Sea simply stated.

"That's a good thing. Why are you so scared to love me?" he asked.

"Because the more I get to know you the more I want to be with you. It would be selfish of me to stay. You deserve much better than me. Someone who can give you everything you desire and deserve."

"I don't understand. You love me but now you want to leave. That makes no sense, Sea. I don't buy it. There's something you're not telling me."

"I will tell you this, Mitch. It has to do with the reason why we haven't had sex yet. I want to be with you sexually more than anything but there are things about my past that I'm not ready to talk about. I thought I was."

"What's the problem? You don't trust me or are you a coward?" Mitch's heart was pounding out of his chest. He didn't want Sea to break up with him.

"I'm a coward. You deserve better than me. I know you have strong feelings for me and I care about you too much to let this go on any further."

"So you're saying because you love me, you're breaking up with me? You're right. You are a coward." Mitch said angrily. "If you really loved me, you would trust me to hear and accept anything you had to say."

Sea began to cry. "If I told you and you left me, I would die. If I told you and you stayed, I would die. I can't win. At least this way it's on my terms. I can't let another man hurt me like Trevor did. I didn't know I would feel this way until I fell for you. I never meant to hurt you. You're a wonderful man, Mitch."

"This doesn't feel right. Are you seeing someone else? Someone you can just fuck and not care about."

"No! It's nothing like that. I really like you. I do. You deserve better than me though."

"Why do you keep saying that? What's wrong with you? Why do I deserve better than you? There is nothing wrong with you. You're perfect." Mitch was confused—now, more than ever. "Just tell me the truth! Who is he? I knew this relationship was too good to be true."

Sea couldn't stop crying.

Through her tears she said, "Meeting Tommy made me realize how serious we were and how much you want me a part of your life.

I was selfish. I shouldn't have kissed you that day in the park and led you on. You're a great person and I couldn't see my life without you, but there are things about me I'm not ready to tell you yet. If you knew the truth, you wouldn't want me and I don't want to be hurt either."

Mitch was bewildered. "Are you a man or hermaphrodite? Do you have STDs or AIDS? Is that why we haven't had sex yet?"

"No. No. Nothing like that," Sea quickly assured him.

"Then what is it? What are you not telling me?" Mitch was desperate. He wanted to know what she was hiding from him.

"Are you married? Are you hiding at your aunt's place to get away from your husband?" Mitch asked.

"No. I'm not married, Mitch. I'm not dying either. I know you desperately want to know but I'm too afraid."

She didn't want to hurt the one person who made her feel special and loved. She put her hands over her face to hide her tears and shame. Sea didn't want to be cruel, but she didn't want to keep Mitch from having the life he deserved. He had so little family that she felt he deserved a family of his own one day and she couldn't provide that. It was a huge decision. She knew that he would give it all up for her and she didn't want that.

"Sea, if you don't trust me enough to tell me what is going on, then it's over. You need to get your things and leave. I don't want you here anymore." Mitch was beside himself. "I'll call Bridget to come get you."

Sea slowly got out of bed to put her shoes on. She was still somewhat inebriated so she was having a tough time balancing herself. Mitch grabbed her by the elbow so she wouldn't fall over. He sat her on the couch to wait for her aunt. Mitch grabbed her jacket and purse and tossed them in her lap. Sea started to cry again. Bridget was at the door a few minutes later. Mitch let her in.

Bridget gathered up Sea's things and helped her out of the apartment. Sea looked back at Mitch and said, "I'm so sorry, Mitch. I wish it didn't have to be like this. I do love you whether you believe me or not."

"None of that matters now, does it?" Mitch said, as he closed the door.

CHAPTER TWELVE

"Hi, Sarah." Sea said, as her sister opened the front door.

Sarah hugged her sister. "It's great to see you. I've missed you."

"I know. I'm sorry about that. I've missed you too Sis."

Sarah helped Sea bring her things in from the car and led her to the guest bedroom. Sarah and Maxwell had moved into a new home since Sea had last seen them. Their new house was bigger than their previous one. It had five bedrooms and two and a half bathrooms; a large kitchen with granite countertops and an island; a two car garage; and a finished basement. The guest bedroom had a greenish blue theme to it. Sea adored it.

Sea and her sister sat down for a cup of tea.

"How are the boys?" Sea asked.

"They're doing really well. Jacob started kindergarten and Kyle entered the second grade a few weeks ago. My boys are growing up so fast."

"Is Kyle interested in sports yet?"

"Yes. He wants to join Little League baseball this year. His friends are all involved so he wants to join, too."

"Wow. That's really great. How about you, Sarah? How have you been?"

"I'm doing okay. I've been tired lately and sick in the morning, but other than that, I'm well." Sarah looked at Sea to search her reaction.

"Are you pregnant, Sarah?"

"Yes. I'll be ten weeks tomorrow."

"Congratulations!" Sea stood up to give her sister a hug. She was truly happy for her.

"Thanks. I wasn't sure how you would react."

"I'm fine. I'm very happy for you and Maxwell. I'm going to have another niece or nephew. Do you hope it's a girl this time?"

"Yes. I really want my little girl. My boys are great but it would be nice to have a little girl to dress up."

"Would you like to see the nursery?" Sarah asked.

"Sure…" Sea said hesitantly.

As they worked their way up the stairs and toward the nursery, Sarah's stomach lurched and she quickly ran to the bathroom to vomit. Sarah left the bathroom a few moments later to continue down the hall. Sea felt bad for her.

"Here it is." Sarah announced. "We finished decorating two days ago. What do you think?"

"It's really great, Sis. I love the colors," Sea said, as she began to tear up.

"What is it, Sea? Don't cry. Let's go back down stairs. I shouldn't have brought you up here. I'm sorry. I wasn't even thinking."

"It's okay. I want to be supportive but it's hard, it hurts to think I'll never have a child of my own someday. I just broke up with my boyfriend because of it. He is the sweetest man I've ever known, and I went and ruined it. I'll never find someone like him again."

"Is this the reason why you came down here, Sea?" her sister asked. "Are you running from your problems again? It's not healthy. Please see a therapist. You can't go through this alone. If not for yourself, do it for me."

"I will think about it. I really don't like therapists though. It's embarrassing and they remind me of Mom."

"I understand that, but you can't keep running from your problems either." Sarah chided.

"I don't want to argue about this, Sarah. I didn't come down here to get reprimanded by you. I needed some time away. I will go back. I'm only here for a week, let's not fight the whole time."

"Okay. I'll let it go for now, but know I only say these things out of love. I hate to see you hurting like this, and to be so powerless over it. I love you Sis."

"I love you too, Sarah. Go gather the boys. Let's go out for some ice cream."

*

Mitch was having a difficult time concentrating at work. It had been forty-eight hours since he last talked to Sea. He couldn't stop thinking about her and what she was hiding from him. He was mystified.

Mitch decided he would drop by Bridget's place after work, to see if she knew anything.

"Hey, Mitch." Bridget said surprised. "I wasn't expecting you today."

"I know. I wanted to talk to you about Sea. I noticed her car wasn't here. Did she go somewhere after work?" he asked.

"After you two split, Sea decided to spend a week in Maryland with her sister. She said she needed to get away and think." Bridget replied.

"I'm so confused, Bridget. Everything was going great between us. Then all of a sudden, she didn't want to be with me anymore. Has she told you anything? What happened to her, before she moved up here?"

"Come, sit down Mitch. I'll make you some coffee. But, it's not my place to tell you what happened."

"So something did happen?"

"Yes." Bridget answered. "I'm sorry I can't be more helpful, but she will tell you when she's ready."

"None of this makes any sense. She's the one who initiated the relationship. She kissed me. Does she enjoy messing with guys heads?"

"No. I don't think so, Mitch. She's obviously confused. I personally think she really likes you, but is too scared to continue on. Her fiancé broke her heart. She doesn't want to get hurt again."

"Why does she think I would hurt her? I've been nothing but nice to her. I would do anything for her."

"She knows you're a great guy, that's why she wanted to be with you. It's hard for her to let go of the past, because it also affects her future. I've said too much already."

"Too much! I'm more confused than ever now. Why can't you just tell me? All this secrecy is stupid. It doesn't help anyone."

"You're right. She should tell you, but give her time. She's not ready yet. Be patient."

"I'm not sure how long I can wait, or if I want to. If she can't trust me with whatever this big secret is, then she doesn't know me very well. I want to be with someone who can trust me and love me for me, without playing games."

"I'm sorry you have to go through this, Mitch. You're a good person. If it's any consolation, I trust you whole heartedly. I trust you with my life and I love you very much."

Mitch smiled. "I know and I love you too, Bridget. I'm going to go. Thanks for the coffee. I'll see myself out."

Mitch kissed her softly on the cheek and left. Bridget shook her head as she watched him go. She was beside herself. She wanted to tell him everything, but she couldn't. It wasn't her place.

*

Sea cooked dinner for the boys the second evening she was there, as Sarah lay down to rest. Sea enjoyed cooking. She used to cook with her father when she was younger. Her mother was always home late from work so her father was in charge of making the family meals. Sea and her father didn't mind, though. They loved it. It was their time together.

"When will dinner be ready Aunt Sea? Kyle asked.

"About another fifteen minutes." she replied. "Why don't you get your brother and go outside and play catch?"

"Do I have to?" Kyle whined.

"It would be good of you to spend time with your brother, instead of playing video games." Sea remarked.

"Mom lets me play video games." Kyle countered.

"Well, your mom is not feeling well right now and she put me in charge. It's really not that big of a deal. Go spend some time with your brother. Don't you realize he idolizes you? I'm not asking for a whole lot here. It's only for fifteen minutes, Kyle. Scoot!"

Kyle finally gave in and went to get his little brother to play catch. Jacob was delighted that his big brother asked him to play. He rarely did. About twelve minutes later, their father came home from work and they all piled into the kitchen.

As Maxwell strolled into the kitchen he asked, "What's for dinner? I'm starving."

"We're having spaghetti tonight. I hope you all are hungry. I made plenty."

Sea tried to stay the whole week but after five days she wanted to get back home. She loved seeing her sister and nephews but it was hard to spend time with them. She wanted what her sister had—family of her own. And, she wanted to get back home to talk to Mitch. She missed him and was impatient. She really wanted to smooth things over with him. She hated how things had ended. It was awful for her, to watch him shut the door in her face. Sea was desperate to see him again and apologize for her behavior.

CHAPTER THIRTEEN

From a distance, Mitch could hear commotion coming from the front desk. He tried to get back to what he was doing, but he couldn't concentrate. He thought the voice sounded familiar. He went to the front to investigate the situation.

"Please! I need to speak with him for just a minute." the woman in distress said.

The receptionist, who was a temp, had strict orders not to let anyone in without an appointment.

"No! I'm sorry ma'am, but I can't let you talk to Mr. Anderson without an appointment. If you don't leave, I'm going to have to call security."

"Don't be ridiculous! I'm his ex-girlfriend. He knows who I am. There's no need to call security. Can you at least call him and tell him I'm here."

"You can put the phone down, Megan. I know her. I'll take care of it from here." Mitch said, as he walked up to the front desk.

The receptionist slowly put the phone down as Mitch approached

Sea. "What are you doing here, Sea? I thought you were in Maryland."

"I was. Is there somewhere we can talk in private?"

"Yes. Follow me." Mitch led her to one of the storage rooms.

Mitch spoke first. "You can't come barging into my place of work and expect everything to be like it was. You shouldn't be here. I have to focus on my work."

"I know. I had to see you, though. I feel horrible about what happened. I still care for you, Mitch."

"You have a funny way of showing it." Mitch said with disdain. "If you care about me, you'll tell me what the hell is going on."

Sea hesitated, debated whether or not to tell him. "I'm sorry, I can't. I came back from my vacation because I wanted to apologize. I shouldn't have kissed you that day in the park and I shouldn't have led you on. You're a great guy. I feel sick to my stomach with how much I hurt you. Any girl would be lucky to have you."

"None of this makes any sense. You sound stupid right now. If you like me, then why did you break up with me? No one does that." Mitch was getting very agitated and wanted to finish the conversation.

"It's very complicated. I know if I tell you, you won't want to be with me."

Mitch chuckled and shook his head. "I have news for you, Sea; I don't want to be with you. You've already ruined whatever relationship we had by breaking up with me. You are selfish and immature. You don't trust me to handle whatever it is you're so afraid to tell me. It doesn't matter at this point because I don't want to be with you." Mitch opened the door and motioned for her to leave and said, "Don't come here again."

After work, Mitch headed to Tommy's place to blow off steam. On the way there, he picked up a twelve pack of beer. When Mitch arrived, Tommy couldn't answer the door because he was in the middle of an intense video game.

"One second, I'm almost done killing zombies." Tommy yelled from the other side of the door.

"I don't care Tommy. Open the door. I have a twelve pack of beer I'm holding in my hands. Hurry up!"

"Okay! Okay! I'm coming!" Tommy stopped the game and went to the door to let Mitch in.

"Hey, Mitch! What's going on? Hard day at work?" Tommy asked as he closed the door.

Mitch told Tommy about Sea visiting him at work earlier that day.

"Sea has no idea what she's done to me. She apologized but I hate her. She plays stupid head games. She needs to be upfront about everything. Life would be much easier that way." Mitch looked at Tommy for a response.

"Who cares? There's other fish in the sea."

They both laughed. "Great pun Tommy. But, Sea is one of a kind, or at least I use to think she was. I was beginning to fall for her and then out of nowhere she breaks up with me. Her looks can only get her so far. There aren't many out there like her. Why did she have to go and fuck everything up?"

"I don't know man. Women are strange creatures. You never know what they're going to do."

"Isn't that the truth?" Mitch said, as he clinked his beer bottle with Tommy's.

"Why don't you come to Las Vegas with me next weekend? It will be a blast. I'm sure my friends won't mind one more person tagging along. Maybe we could get you laid while we're there. It's legal you know."

Mitch groaned. "Thanks, but no. I'm not up for partying much. I would be a drag. I told Bridget I'd be over next weekend to help fix her bathroom tiles. Besides, I might be able to get it out of her why Sea is acting so strange."

"Well I hope you do, because you're in a pretty sad state," Tommy said.

After a couple of hours playing video games on the Xbox, Mitch left.

*

"Sea, can you come here for a minute, please?" Bridget called out to her while she stood in the kitchen making dinner.

"Be right there Aunt Bridget?" Sea replied. A few moments later Sea walked into the kitchen.

"What's up?"

"Mitch will be here this weekend to fix the tiles in my bathroom and I was hoping you could make yourself scarce on Saturday. I'd really appreciate it. Mitch needs to have his space and I don't want you to upset him while he's here helping me. I don't want him to feel like he can't visit me anymore."

"That's fine. I understand." Sea felt a twinge in her stomach and went back into the living room.

*

Mitch arrived early on Saturday morning to start working on Bridget's bathroom.

"Thanks for coming over Mitch. I don't know what I would do without you," Bridget said.

"It's no problem at all, Bridget. I never mind helping you. I'd love some coffee, if you have some."

"It's almost done brewing. I knew you'd want some."

"Where's Sea?"

"I asked her to stay upstairs today while you're here so you could focus."

"Thanks. I was a little worried about that. I don't think I could handle seeing her today. Did you get all the supplies I asked for?"

"I bought everything on the list you gave me. I hope it's all the right stuff though."

"Okay. I'll go ahead and get started while I'm waiting for the coffee to finish brewing." Mitch left the kitchen and began working on the bathroom. A few minutes later, he heard Bridget cursing in the kitchen. Mitch became curious, when she kept it up. He found her fuming over the microwave.

"What's wrong Bridget?"

"I can't remember how to use this wretched thing."

"What do you mean? You've been using microwaves for thirty years."

"I know. It's strange. I should know how to use it, but I can't seem to remember how. It must be old age. My memory is not what it used to be."

"Maybe you should go see the doctor about it. You're only sixty-five. It's not like you're trying to learn something new."

"Yeah. Maybe."

He shrugged it off and went back to work in the bathroom. Mitch wondered if he should talk to Sea about it, but he wasn't ready to see her yet. He needed more time.

Sea didn't want to disobey her aunt's wishes, but she wanted to talk to Mitch. She paced back and forth in her bedroom trying to figure out what to say to him. What could she say? She broke his heart and that's not an easy thing to repair. She slumped back down onto her bed. There really wasn't anything else she could say or do except to leave him alone.

CHAPTER FOURTEEN

Sea was continually in Mitch's thoughts. He loved her, but there was no future with her. He didn't understand why she couldn't be honest with him when they were such good friends. He had never given her a reason not to trust him.

Mitch wanted to move on with his life so he set up a profile on an online dating service. He registered on the site, then began looking through all the female profiles. He wanted to find someone he could relate to and who was relatively good looking. He knew now that looks could be deceiving. He meticulously looked through all the pictures and profiles. Mitch hoped to find someone whom he could settle down with. He was not getting any younger and he wanted his dad to experience the joy of having grandkids. Mitch didn't want to live the bachelor life forever.

Finally, after an hour of looking, he found her. She had long brown hair, blue eyes and a nice face. Her name was Molly. She was not as pretty as Sea but Mitch liked her. He was impressed by her profile. She was a fifth grade school teacher who liked to watch science fiction movies and play board games. She was born in Virginia but grew up in California. She moved to Springfield, Massachusetts after she graduated college. Mitch emailed her. He asked if she wanted to get together for coffee sometime. Thirty minutes later, he got a response—she wanted to meet him. He emailed her back and suggested they meet on Monday morning for coffee. Monday was a national holiday and they both wouldn't be working. Molly emailed back and confirmed. Mitch finally had a date and he was excited to meet someone new.

As Mitch waited in the coffee house for Molly to arrive, his palms started to sweat and his right leg wouldn't stop bouncing up and down. When she finally arrived, he was slightly disappointed. She had fibbed somewhat about her weight. Molly was about twenty pounds heavier than she had admitted to, but at least her curves were in proportion. She was dressed appropriately and her smile radiated.

Mitch stood up to shake her hand. "Hi! I'm Mitch. Are you Molly?"

"Yes. I'm Molly. It's great to meet you Mitch."

Mitch pulled out her chair for her.

"Oh, thank you Mitch. What a gentlemen." Molly sat down and put her purse underneath the table.

"I ordered you a coffee already. I hope that's okay?"

"That's perfect. I like my coffee black."

Mitch felt awkward and uncomfortable but wasn't sure why.

"You have a pretty smile."

"Thanks."

They spent about two hours talking, learning about one another.

They truly seemed to be enjoying each other's company. Mitch appreciated her forthright approach to meeting new people. He thought it was refreshing but felt somewhat exposed. Molly adored his witty remarks and conversational skills. He seemed willing to tell her anything. She liked that about him. She had a tendency to stare at times, and she loved his green eyes. At the end of their date, they decided to meet again soon.

*

Sea avoided Mitch whenever he came to the house, for Bridget's sake. She didn't want Bridget to suffer for her mistakes. She tried to move on with her life and accept that she would never be with Mitch. She took her sister's advice and began seeing a therapist again. She put forth the effort during the sessions, but weeks without talking to Mitch were difficult. She missed her friend immensely.

After about a month, Sea noticed that Mitch didn't come around as often as before. He was engaged in other activities but she didn't know what. She wasn't sure she wanted to know. He was free to date other women but she would rather he didn't. Of course she had no say in the matter, but she didn't want competition. Sea had several guys ask her out but she wasn't interested in just any guy anymore. She wanted Mitch. She loved him. He showed her how a girl should be treated. The worst decision she ever made was breaking up with him. He was the man she wanted to spend the rest of her life with.

*

After about two months of dating, Mitch decided to introduce Molly to Bridget. Bridget planned a big dinner for Mitch and his new girlfriend. He invited his father and Tommy so they could meet her, too.

"It's nice to finally meet you. I've heard a lot about you," Molly said.

"All good things I hope." Bridget teased.

"Of course!" Molly answered right away.

Mitch's father and best friend finally arrived and he introduced them to Molly.

Michael put his coat away and then walked over and gave Bridget a hug.

After a few minutes, Sea came downstairs to check out Mitch's new girlfriend. She wasn't invited to the dinner for obvious reasons. She overdressed for the occasion. She wanted to outshine Molly and impress Mitch, which wasn't very hard. Sea looked amazing but Mitch paid no attention. She was disappointed when he didn't look her way. Sea was very attractive but she felt insecure now that Mitch was moving on. She was jealous but tried not to show it. She made sure she didn't give Mitch much eye contact, but it couldn't be avoided when he introduced her to Molly—as Bridget's niece. He was callous about it, proving that he was over her and clearly moving on. It stung, but she knew it was her fault they weren't together anymore. She wanted him back but didn't know how.

"Dinner time!" Bridget yelled.

"You're not staying are you?" Bridget whispered to Sea. "No.

I'm going out with a friend from work."

"Okay. Good. I know this may be difficult for you but tonight is for Mitch and Molly. There would be too much tension in the air if you stayed."

"I know. I'm leaving. I just wanted to meet her first."

She watched everyone gather at the table and fill their plates with food. Her Aunt Bridget always made the best meals. It was a shame she couldn't stay. She loved her cooking. That night, it was Mexican food. Bridget made it especially for Mitch, it was his favorite.

Sea ran back upstairs to change. She really did overdress for just dinner and a movie with a friend.

"Bye Aunt Bridget! I'll be back around midnight. Don't wait up. It was nice to meet you Molly," she said, as she grabbed her purse and walked out the front door.

"This food looks great Bridget. Thanks for going through the trouble of making it." Mitch said.

"It was my pleasure Mitch."

Molly took the first bite. The food she tasted was so salty she had to spit her food out onto her napkin.

Molly leaned over and whispered to Mitch. "Does Bridget usually put a lot of salt into her food?"

He looked at her inquisitively and said, "No. Why?"

"Taste it."

When he did, he spit it into his napkin too. A few seconds later, Tommy did the same thing, followed by Michael and Bridget.

Bridget had a look of disbelief and curiosity as to why or how she put so much salt in. She had no memory of putting that much in.

"I'm so sorry, everyone. I'm not sure what happened. I honestly don't remember putting that much salt in. I'll go ahead and order pizza. Again, I'm very sorry."

"It's okay. Things happen." But as Mitch said this he wondered if something was really going on. He recalled when she couldn't remember how to use the microwave. It was strange. Was she ill? Was it a fluke? Should he worry? He was definitely going to keep an eye on her.

"Has this happened to you before Bridget?" Michael asked.

"No. Never." she answered. "Not that I can recall, but my memory isn't what it used to be these days."

"When's the last time you received a full check-up?" Michael asked.

"We can talk about that later. I'm sure Molly doesn't want to listen to this silly conversation. Let's not focus on me. So what's it like being a school teacher Molly?"

Michael was annoyed that she had changed the subject. Bridget had never been the type of person to worry about her health and preferred not to go to the doctor if she could help it. Michael would let this drop for now but he was going to finish this conversation later.

"It's great. I love my job. I've wanted to be a teacher ever since I was a little girl. My mom and dad are professors at Stanford so I guess it's only natural that I became a teacher."

"Oh really? What do they teach?" Bridget asked.

"My dad teaches 'Critical Theory' and my mom teaches 'Environmental Justice'."

"That sounds very interesting. Good for them." Bridget said.

"Yeah, I'm very proud of my parents. They instilled in me a very good work ethic. They think it's great that I'm teaching children. They know that's where the knowledge all starts. Plant those necessary seeds for a good life. Unfortunately, the county school system puts too much focus on test scores and not enough on the individual child. Pulling the music program and physical education in our school has been devastating for the children."

After waiting forty minutes for the pizza to arrive, everyone was starving. Bridget grabbed the paper plates and they all sat back down to eat.

"I am famished. I was about to eat my left arm if I didn't get any food soon." Tommy joked.

"I don't think there was any danger of you withering away, Tommy." Mitch added.

"I'm stuffed. I think we better start heading out, it's getting late. Thank you for a lovely evening Bridget and don't worry about the mishap." Mitch said.

"Yes. Thank you for having me and it was great to meet you all." Molly said.

As they were walking out of the house, Molly said, "Sea is really pretty. Did you two ever date?"

Mitch hesitated before responding. "Yes, but it didn't work out. She broke up with me and wouldn't tell me why. We don't talk much anymore."

"That explains why you were so cold."

"I wasn't that bad, was I?"

"Yes you were. I'm curious to know why she broke up with you though. You're quite the catch."

Mitch smiled. "Thanks."

"You have no idea what she's hiding?"

"No. I don't. She refuses to tell me. I asked Bridget but she wouldn't tell me much. She didn't want to tell me more since it wasn't her place."

"That's so strange," she said.

"I know. It is. I asked Sea several questions and she said no to all of them. She's not married. Not dying. Not a man. Not a hermaphrodite. No other boyfriend that I know of. We got along great in the beginning but once it started to get serious she called it quits. I think something happened in her past that she's not ready to face. That much I got from Bridget."

"You actually asked her if she was a hermaphrodite?"

"Yes. I did. We never had sex so I figured it may have something to do with body parts. Why do you want to know all of this?"

"I'm a curious creature. Sounds like a piece of a mystery novel to me."

Mitch looked pensive as she was talking.

"I'd rather not think about her anymore." Mitch said with a serious tone.

"I'd rather think about Bridget. She's not acting herself lately. I'm worried."

"I know you probably don't want to, but have you thought about asking Sea? See if she has noticed anything unusual. She does live with her. She would be the perfect person to ask."

"I know. I've thought about asking her, but I'm not ready to speak to her. It may be nothing. If something else happens, I'll talk to her."

"Do you want to spend the night at my place?" Molly asked.

"I would love to but I have a lot on my mind and I wouldn't be much fun to be around. I'm sorry." Mitch replied.

"It's okay. Another night."

CHAPTER FIFTEEN

Sea awoke early one Saturday morning from loud noises that were coming from downstairs. She put on her bathrobe and went downstairs to find out what the commotion was about. She found her aunt, flinging clothes and under garments everywhere.

"What's going on? Why are you up so early, Aunt Bridget?" Sea asked.

"I have a date tonight. I'm trying to find the clothes I just bought. I can't find my lipstick either. Did you take it?"

"No. I didn't know you had a date with Michael."

"I don't. It's with Robert."

Sea looked confused. "Who's Robert?"

"A man I met at the bar last night."

"How long have you been going to the bar?"

"A few days. I want to feel young again. I'm tired of being cooped up in this house. You're not the only one who can have fun."

"Are you making fun of me?"

"No. Why would you say that?"

"You just seem out of character that's all. Does Michael know you're dating?"

"No. I don't need his permission either. We may be good friends but I'm my own woman, I can make my own decisions."

*

"I had fun last night, Mitch."

"Me too, Molly. I'm glad we met."

"Why? Because of last night?"

"No. Well. Yes. But that's not the only reason. You're a good person. You have a kind heart, you're easy to talk to and you have a beautiful smile."

Molly smiled and said, "You're not so bad yourself."

Mitch moved his arm over and held Molly's head on his shoulder. They snuggled for about an hour more.

"You want to hang out tonight?" Mitch asked.

"Sure. Where would you like to go?" Molly answered.

"How about that nice Bar & Grill in town?"

"Okay. Pick me up at five o'clock."

"I'll be here." Mitch got up from the bed to take a shower. It was a Saturday but he had to go in to work for a few hours.

*

When Sea arrived home from running her usual weekend errands, her aunt wasn't home. Sea found that odd—her aunt rarely went out, and when she did, she would leave Sea a note or tell her ahead of time. Because of her strange behavior that morning, Sea decided that her aunt must have gone to the bar early to wait for her date there. Curious about her aunt's new beau, she drove to the Bar & Grill.

At first, Sea couldn't find her but as she looked closer, she spotted her sitting at the bar drinking a beer. Bridget's appearance shocked her. She was wearing a lot of make-up. She had on a mini skirt and a halter top, an outfit a twenty-year-old would wear. Something was definitely not right with her aunt. Wanting to see who she was meeting, without disturbing her, she sat out of sight nearby.

After twenty minutes, she saw Mitch and Molly walk in. They didn't notice her or Bridget so she relaxed. After another five minutes, a man walked in who looked about forty-five. He walked over to the bar area and greeted Bridget with a hug. At twenty years her junior, he was an odd match for her aunt. That did not feel right to her. She needed to talk to someone. She didn't want to interrupt Mitch on his date with Molly. She called Michael, who arrived quickly. Sea met him at the doorway.

"Where is she? I don't see her." Michael said.

"She's over at the bar."

Just then, Mitch noticed his father standing at the front of the restaurant talking to Sea. He saw her point in the direction of the bar. He looked over at the bar area and noticed an older woman dressed provocatively. Mitch didn't recognize her at first but when she looked in his direction he realized who it was. He was shocked to see her dressed like that. His earlier concerns were now confirmed. There was something definitely amiss with Bridget.

Mitch excused himself and made his way swiftly to Michael.

"Dad! What's going on? Why is Bridget dressed like that?"

"I don't know. Sea called me to come and check out the situation."

"Sea, is this the first time you've noticed anything strange going on with Bridget?" Mitch asked.

"No. She has been acting strange for a while now. She has been forgetting about important orders she needs to fill and customers have called complaining about her work. That is very unusual for her. I just assumed she was overwhelmed and stressed. I had no idea it was this extreme. She hardly ever wakes before eight. She's very routine about her day. This morning she was up at six o'clock looking for stuff and making a lot of noise. She woke me up. She's never done that before. She said she met a man named Robert and that she had a date with him tonight. She was looking for clothes to wear for her date. And her lipstick. She never wears lipstick."

"She did when she was younger." Michael said.

"Have you ever noticed anything, Mitch?" Sea asked.

"A couple of things. The day I came over to fix the tile in the bathroom, she made a big fuss about how to use the microwave. It was strange. And then the salt incident."

"The salt incident?" Sea asked.

"The day that Bridget made dinner for Mitch and Molly, Bridget put too much salt in the food. She had no recollection that she had done it. She was just as surprised as everyone else when she ate it." Michael said.

"When Dad asked her, 'When was the last time you went to the doctor?' she dismissed him."

Michael made his way over to the bar. "Hi, Bridget."

"What are you doing here?" she asked.

"Sea called me," he replied.

And then to Robert, "Take a hike."

"What are you doing? You can't do that. He's my friend. I want him here."

"No, he's not. He's using you to get himself drinks and probably other things too. You're twenty years older than he is. Think about it."

Robert looked uncomfortable. "Whatever. I'm out of here. I don't need this."

"No. Don't leave. Robert! Stay! Don't you like me?"

Robert ignored her and left.

The bartender approached and said, "Your friend is right, ma'am. That guy was using you, sorry to say. I see him in here all the time using older women to buy him drinks."

Bridget looked deflated and sad. "I really thought he liked me."

"What are you doing picking men up at a bar, anyway? What has gotten into you? Why are you acting so strange?" Michael demanded.

"I'm fine. He's gone. You can leave me alone now. I want to finish my drink."

"You need to go see the doctor Bridget. You're not well." Michael said.

"I'm fine Michael. I just need a vacation. I've been working too hard lately. I'll be fine."

Michael didn't want to upset her any further, so he left. Mitch sat back down when his food arrived. Sea stayed at the bar with her aunt until she was ready to leave.

"What was that all about?" Molly asked.

"Oh, nothing. Everything is fine now." he answered.

"When I saw you talking to Sea... your face lit up." Molly observed.

"It did?" Mitch said in disbelief. "It didn't mean anything. I was surprised to see her here, that's all. I don't want to be with her. I'm here with you. I like you."

"Honest?" she asked.

"Yes. Honestly," he responded.

Molly wanted to believe him.

CHAPTER SIXTEEN

A woman from behind him called out. "Hey, Tommy!" Tommy turned around to see who it was.

"Molly? I didn't know you were a member here."

"Yeah, I've been coming here for about two years now."

"Mitch never mentioned you went to the gym."

"I never told him." Molly said. "I didn't want him to know. I've lost a lot of weight since college and it's not something I want to tell people. I plan to tell him someday but not now. Please don't say anything."

"It's none of my business," Tommy said. "My lips are sealed."

"Thanks."

"I never thought I'd bump into you here." Molly admitted. "Glad to see you're trying to get fit."

"I know, right! To tell you the truth, I was hoping to meet a girl. I found one, but she's already taken."

"Oh, really. Who?" Molly said surprised.

Tommy tilted his head and raised an eyebrow. Molly blushed and said, "Oh."

Molly put her gym bag on her shoulder and said, "Well… have fun! I was about to leave when I saw you. I've been here for about two hours now. I usually get here around seven in the morning, if you ever want to work out together."

"That would be great!" Tommy responded. "I have no idea what I'm doing."

"To start with, I would recommend going on the treadmill, first on a low speed, and then do a couple of weight repetitions for your arms. Don't do too much your first day or you won't want to come back." Molly said with a giggle.

"Thanks for the tip. See you later." Tommy said.

*

Three months after Tommy started going to the gym, he began meeting Molly at a coffee shop around the corner before they began their workout. Molly watched his mouth as he talked about his friendship with Mitch. His face had changed slightly after losing thirty-five pounds. Molly realized how comfortable she felt around him and that she looked forward to seeing him every other weekday morning. She could say anything to him and not feel judged for it because he knew what it was like to be overweight. Tommy noticed that she was staring at him.

"Do I have something on my face?" he asked.

"No." Molly giggled. "Come on. We better get going. We can't talk all morning. The gym is calling our names."

Tommy let out a sigh.

*

On her way to work, Sea dropped by the gas station to fill her tank. When she swiped her credit card, she looked up and noticed Molly and Tommy walking out of the coffee shop across the street. She couldn't believe her eyes. She watched where they went. They both entered a gym nearby. She finished up at the pump and parked her car at the gym parking lot. She sat in her car and debated whether or not to confront them. The clock ticked by. Sea continued to sit there, even though she was officially late for work. She finally decided to go in. She would watch them from afar to see what they were up to. Was Molly cheating on Mitch?

*

Molly exited the bathroom after changing into her gym clothes and Tommy was waiting for her along the wall. He noticed how slim she had become when he saw her in a new tight fitting outfit. He became excited. He placed his towel in front of himself so she wouldn't notice anything. Tommy watched Molly as she adjusted her shoe. When she looked up, he met her eyes and blushed.

"You made my day, Tommy," she said with a grin.

"How's that?" he said surprised.

"No one has ever looked at me the way you just did. You make me feel beautiful."

"You are!" he said, as he blushed again.

"It's so cute when you blush Tommy. It's how I know you're not lying. I hate when guys lie to me, to make me feel better about myself, but you don't. With you, it's real." Molly said.

"Molly, I like you, but nothing can happen between us. Mitch is my best friend. I would never steal his girl."

"I was never his Tommy. For a long time I wanted to be. I believe he's still in love with Sea. I can't blame him. She's very beautiful. I hoped he would get over her after some time but he hasn't. In the six months that we've been dating, he's never looked at me the way he looks at her. I'm so tired of it. I was going to break it off this weekend. I like you, Tommy."

Tommy was speechless for a moment.

"I have to talk to Mitch first. I can't see you behind his back."

"I understand." Molly said. "But, I don't want to waste any more time. I'm not going to wait until the weekend. I'm going to break it off with him tonight."

"Are you sure this is what you want? Mitch is better looking than me. I'm just a sack of potatoes compared to him."

"I'm sure. His heart is already taken and I found someone who has captured mine. When I see something I like, I'm going to go for it. No more hesitating."

Tommy smiled broadly. He moved forward to hug her but suddenly Sea was there, pushing him aside, yelling, "Tommy! How dare you! How can you betray your best friend like that? And Molly, you whore! Mitch trusted you!"

Whack! Sea slapped Molly across the face.

"What is wrong with you, Sea? Molly demanded, massaging her reddened cheek.

Tommy stood there in shock. He couldn't believe what he had just seen.

An employee of the gym went to grab an ice pack and call the police.

Sea turned to Tommy again and said, "You need to tell Mitch what's going on or I will."

"Nothing is going on, Sea. Molly and I are just friends. I would never do anything to hurt Mitch. Why do you care so much? You broke up with him."

"Just because I broke it off with him doesn't mean I don't care. I want the best for him. I don't want him getting hurt."

"You mean like how you hurt him," Tommy snapped back.

"Don't change the subject. I saw you. You were about to hug her."

The employee returned with the ice pack and warned Sea that the police were on their way. When the police arrived, Molly didn't press charges but asked if they could escort Sea out of the gym. As the police escorted Sea out, she shouted, "You better tell him or I will!" The police continued to escort her out. They walked her to her car and advised her to stay out of trouble. The manager of the gym banned Sea from entering again.

Sea called in sick to work. She sat in her car thinking about how close she came to going to jail. Molly could have easily pressed charges. There were plenty of witnesses. Sea felt awful about what she had done. She knew now that she couldn't escape her feelings for

Mitch. She needed an excuse to take her frustration out but it shouldn't have been by violence. She didn't know what was coming over her. She felt so much pain and loss not having Mitch in her life. She sat there and cried.

CHAPTER SEVENTEEN

"You should have seen it Mitch. It was bizarre. Sea slapped Molly right in the face. I couldn't believe my eyes. That girl is still crazy for you."

"Are you serious?" Mitch asked. "Sea slapped Molly? Why? Is she okay?"

"Yeah. Molly's fine. Her face will probably sting for a day or two. She went home to ice it."

"So why did Sea slap her?"

"Well... that's the other thing I came over here to talk to you about. How do I say this?"

"Just say it."

"I have feelings for Molly."

"You dog. When and how did this happen?"

"You're not mad?"

"Not really," Mitch said. "I like Molly but it's not the same as when I was with Sea. I think Sea has ruined me forever. That girl is something else."

"So how come you haven't broken it off with Molly yet?"

"Because I know she really likes me and I didn't want to hurt her feelings. She's a great girl and very smart. And, she was a nice distraction for me. I didn't want to be thinking about Sea all the time, like before."

"Dude, that's not right." Tommy chided. "And anyway, she doesn't like you as much as you might think." he added.

"What do you mean by that?"

"She told me she was going to break up with you tonight."

Mitch cocked his head to the side. "You're lying."

Tommy looked straight at him. "I'm being dead serious man. That's what she told me. We've been going to the same gym for the past few months and I've really gotten to know her. Sea slapped her because she saw me moving in for a hug and she was about to accept it."

Mitch had a concerned look on his face. "You were trying to put moves on my girlfriend. Some friend you are."

"It was going to be a quick friendly hug. I wasn't going to molest her for goodness sake! We both decided to tell you first before anything real started to happen. I wouldn't do that to you. That's why I'm here talking to you about it now."

"I know man. I'm sorry." Mitch said, as he sat down on his couch, his ego bruised. "So you really like her, eh?"

"I do. Come to find out, we have a lot in common. She even said I make her feel beautiful, which she is. I like my girls to have some meat on their bones. I'm not sure what she sees in me though."

"Come off it. You're a great person Tommy. That's why we're

best friends. You may burp and fart a little too much for my comfort, but you're my right hand man."

"Thanks dude. You think you'll talk to Sea?" Tommy asked. "Find out why she's acting so crazy?"

"I don't know. I am going to talk to Molly later and apologize for my ex's behavior. I feel bad she got involved in this. I want to make sure she's okay."

Mitch's nose started to wrinkle from disgust. "Tommy! Seriously? Now?"

"Sorry man, I couldn't hold it in any longer."

Mitch threw a couch pillow at him.

*

The next day, Mitch dropped by Molly's place after work. She invited him in. As soon as Mitch stepped into her apartment he started talking.

"I'm really sorry that you got mixed up into our drama. That Sea slapped you. I'm surprised she would do something like that." He paused for a few seconds to allow Molly to respond. Molly took a moment to collect her thoughts.

"In a way, I'm glad she slapped me. Not that I enjoy pain, but it confirms my opinion about you and Sea. She obviously still loves you."

"Tommy said the same thing."

"He's right." Molly simply stated. "You still love her too. Don't you?" Mitch ignored her.

"I was shocked when Tommy told me what happened. He also told me how he feels about you."

"Yes. I know. It's not very fair to you but you haven't been very fair with me either. You're only staying with me because you're trying to forget about Sea. I'm not stupid, just lonely. I don't want to hurt you, Mitch, but I like Tommy. He makes me happy and you don't. I'm breaking up with you."

"I deserved that." Mitch said. "You are right. I'm not over Sea and I wasn't being fair to you. I hope we can still be friends. You're a great person Molly. I really respect that you two didn't go behind my back and explained it to me in person before anything got too heated."

"Thanks Mitch. That means a lot. I'm glad you recognize everything for what it is and what it isn't. I have no problem continuing to be friends if you don't. That's all we pretty much were in the first place, to be truthful."

"Yeah, I'm sorry about that. I wasn't being very fair. I used you to get over Sea and that wasn't cool. I'm glad you finally found someone who makes you happy."

"Maybe someday you and Sea will be together again—who knows." Molly said as Mitch headed toward the door.

"I highly doubt that." Mitch responded.

Mitch hugged Molly goodbye and left.

*

Mitch wasn't finished. He dropped by Bridget's to talk to Sea. He wanted her to know what was going on so she would leave Molly and Tommy alone. He was so angry with her it was hard for him to maintain his composure. She was selfish and immature in his eyes.

"Hi, Bridget, is Sea here?" Mitch asked.

"Yeah, she's upstairs." Bridget answered.

Mitch walked up the stairs and called out, "Sea!"

"Yes! Mitch is that you?"

"Yeah, I need to talk to you." Mitch yelled back as he made his way up to the third floor.

"So you heard what happened yesterday?"

"Yes I did. You need to apologize to Molly. She was innocent. Tommy told me what really happened and I believe him. They are just friends but they do have feelings for one another. Molly and I have severed ties and I have no problem with them dating. Tommy and Molly deserve to be happy. You need to stay away from her. Got it?" Mitch said bluntly.

Sea winced at his tone. "I got it."

"I have to go. Make sure you apologize to Molly." Mitch said, as he turned to leave.

Sea was hurt by his candor and called out to him. "I did it for you! How was I supposed to know it was innocent?"

Mitch turned around and walked back toward her. "What you did was not heroic, it was stupid. You could have gone to jail. Stay out of my affairs." And with that, Mitch was gone.

*

The next morning, Sea went to Molly's apartment to hand deliver a bouquet of flowers and to apologize for her behavior. Sea knocked on her door. Molly peeked through the peep hole to see who it was.

"Go away Sea or I'm calling the police!" Molly said through the door.

"Wait! I've come to apologize," Sea said quickly. "What I did was wrong and I'm sorry. I brought you some flowers. Please open the door. Mitch explained everything to me and I feel awful. Also… I want to pay for your missed day of work, because of your injury."

Sea heard nothing and waited.

"Really?" Molly said with disbelief. At that, she slowly opened the door.

She poked her head through and said, "Really? You would pay for my missed day of work?"

"Yes. Why not? You didn't press charges. It's the least I can do."

"How much?" Molly asked.

"Will two hundred cover it?"

"Yeah. That sounds good." Molly said and she slowly opened the door.

"Do you have it on you?" Molly asked.

"Yes. It's in my purse." Sea fished through her purse to get her wallet out. "Here."

"Thanks. That will help out a lot. That was a nice gesture, Sea. Would you like some tea?"

"I would love some," she said, as she entered Molly's apartment.

As Molly walked to her cabinet to find a vase for the flowers she turned to Sea and asked, "Can I ask you something personal?"

"Sure. What would you like to know?"

"Are you still in love with Mitch?"

"Oh. Well. It's complicated."

Molly looked at her doubtfully and said, "Doesn't seem that complicated to me. You either love him or you don't. Why are you making life so difficult for yourself? Tell Mitch how you feel."

"You don't even know me. I slap you and you think that gives you license to pry into my life?"

"Yes, I do. I could have pressed charges but I didn't."

"Fine. Whatever. It's not that simple. Nothing I do or say is going to change anything. Mitch hates me. I ruined whatever it was that we had."

"What happened, if you don't mind me asking?" Molly said.

"We fell in love."

Molly chuckled. "You're afraid of love? Everyone deserves to be loved."

Sea let out a sigh. "He's a great guy and deserves someone who can give him everything and I can't do that."

Molly thought about it for a moment and said, "If you love him and he loves you, you both will find a way to make it work because that's what people do when they are in love."

Sea gave her a smile. "You make it sound so simple."

"It is that simple. Everything else is nonsense. You think you're doing the right thing because it's easier than facing the truth. Until you face the truth, you won't be happy. I denied myself so many things because I didn't think I deserved better and I ended up one hundred and fifty pounds overweight in the end. I woke up one morning and decided to believe in myself despite what others thought. I lost a hundred pounds because I finally realized my worth. I broke up with Mitch because I knew he was still in love with someone else and I deserved better."

"Wow. That's really great, Molly. I had no idea. You seem like a really great person. I can't believe I slapped you. Will you forgive me?"

"Sure. I forgive you, but I think you need to apologize to Mitch too. He's really hurting."

"I did but he doesn't care. He won't talk to me. I don't know what to say to him either. I'm not ready to tell him everything."

Sea let out another sigh. She was creating her own havoc. Life was as easy or as hard as you made it be.

"You have to talk to him. He deserves the truth."

"I know, but I'm afraid. My ex-fiancé broke my heart and I'm afraid Mitch will do the same when I tell him the truth."

"I think you underestimate Mitch. Yes, he was with me while he was still in love with you but he didn't know what else to do. He's genuine. The real deal. You can trust him. If you two love each other, it will work out. Trust me."

"How can you be so sure?"

"Because love can do mysterious things."

CHAPTER EIGHTEEN

One morning, Bridget woke up feeling light headed and queasy. She had been feeling a little under the weather for the past few days and assumed it was because she had been working too hard. She had more orders to fill than usual with the holiday season fast approaching. She hadn't thought too much about it since she was getting older and Sea wasn't available to help as much as before. So she had figured it was pure exhaustion that was causing her to feel the way she did. As the morning progressed, she developed a terrible migraine. After she ate some toast and drank a glass of water, she climbed back into bed.

"Why are you still in bed, Aunt Bridget?" Sea asked, as she checked on her aunt, who was usually busy with her day by then.

"It's eleven o'clock. Are you sick? Do you need me to call Michael?" Sea inquired. There was no response. Sea bent down to take a closer look at her aunt. All of a sudden, Bridget began to fidget under the sheets and then started shaking. Sea uncovered her to see what was happening. She could see that her aunt's hands were balled up into fists and her back was arched. Suddenly, it dawned on her that her aunt was having a seizure. To her knowledge, her aunt wasn't epileptic. Sea picked up the phone and called 911. The paramedics arrived twelve minutes later. Sea quickly opened the door and directed them to Bridget's bedroom. After evaluating her and determining she was stable enough for transport, they placed Bridget on the gurney. The paramedics allowed Sea to ride in the ambulance alongside her. Sea called Michael on the way to the hospital so he could meet her there.

"This is not necessary Sea. I'm fine. I'm a little under the weather is all."

Sea scoffed, "A little under the weather? You just had a seizure Aunt Bridget. That's no small thing."

"Really? I thought I just passed out. Explains why I feel more tired now."

"They need to run some tests to find out what's going on. People don't start seizing out of the blue like that unless it's serious."

"I suppose you're right, Sea." Bridget said.

Thirty minutes later, Michael and Mitch arrived at the hospital. There wasn't much for Sea to report to them except that Bridget had had a seizure and now she was in the back getting a battery of tests done.

"Did they say how long it would take?" Michael asked Sea.

"The doctor said it would take about an hour or so to get the results back from the MRI." Sea answered.

Michael walked a few steps away from them and stared out the window.

"Are you okay, Dad?" Mitch asked.

From a distance he said, "No son. I'm not. I'm afraid of losing my best friend. Bridget has always been there for us. I don't want to lose her like I lost your mother. She helped me raise you."

Sea left to go get some coffee and to give them some time alone.

"What's going on between you and Sea? You've been cold as ice to her since we've been here."

"Dad… this isn't the place to talk about it."

"No better time than the present son. Nobody is around and we have an hour of waiting ahead of us. Tell me what's going on. I need something to distract me."

Mitch looked around to see if anyone was within hearing distance.

"Fine. A while ago Sea slapped Molly in the face. She thought Molly was cheating on me with Tommy. She wasn't. It was all a big misunderstanding."

"Wow! She did that for you? Sounds like Sea is still in love with you."

"God help me for saying this, but I still love her. I just don't know what to do with her. I can't escape her. We would be together if she weren't so stubborn. From what I've learned through Bridget, she has some big secret she doesn't think I can handle. It hurts when someone doesn't trust you enough to tell you their deepest secret. Dad, I was in heaven. She is the most beautiful girl I had ever dated and then she ripped my heart out for no reason."

Mitch saw Sea coming back with coffee and decided to go for a walk. She approached them at a quick pace but then slowed down when she saw Mitch leave.

Mitch's father walked over to where Sea was sitting and sat down next to her. "Is that for me?" he asked.

"What?"

Michael pointed to one of the three coffees she had sitting next to her and said, "Is that for me?"

"Oh. Yes. Here. Sorry. My mind was somewhere else."

"Thinking about my son perhaps?" Michael remarked.

"Yes. How did you know?" Sea asked.

"It doesn't take a genius to figure it out. It's pretty obvious. Plus, you looked pretty disappointed when you saw Mitch leave."

"I don't know what to do. He won't talk to me."

"Can you blame him?"

"No…"

"Slapping his girlfriend probably wasn't your finest hour."

"He told you?"

"Yeah, just a few minutes ago."

"You don't hate me?"

"Why should I hate you? You didn't slap me."

Sea stared at him. "I broke your son's heart."

Michael put his arm around her.

"That's between you and my son. You have goodness in you but also a lot of pain; the kind that can cripple a person. Don't let it keep you from being happy. I raised him right. Tell him the truth. He can handle it."

"I'm too scared." she said.

"Life is what you make of it Sea. There were lots of paths I could have followed once my wife died, but I chose to fight those bad feelings and eventually I won. I chose my son and his happiness instead of my own. I wanted to drown my sorrows but I couldn't because I had a son depending on me for everything. I'm so glad I did because he has grown up to be a wonderful human being."

"I know he has, but I don't want to hurt him any more than I already have."

"That's a bad excuse. You need to be honest with yourself. It's time to grow up and be an adult and face adult situations. Life is hard but also rewarding when you're willing to take that risk. So you might get hurt, but at least you tried. Or, life might surprise you and you'll end up insanely happy. You won't know unless you try."

"If he finds out that I can't..."

"You can't what?" Mitch asked from behind.

"Oh... you startled me. I thought you went for a walk?"

"I was going to but I didn't want to venture off too far in case the doctor came back sooner than expected. Don't change the subject. You can't what, Sea?"

"Don't ask me that Mitch, especially not here."

"Why not? You were about to tell my dad right here. You can tell everyone else this big secret you have but not me, the man you supposedly love. Who you even slapped someone for. You don't make any sense. Just tell me. What are you so afraid of? That we will break up. It's too late for that. You beat me to it."

"I... well... um..." Sea wanted to tell him, but her fear crippled her. She didn't know how to tell the man she loved that if he ever took her back, he would never have children of his own.

"He deserves to know Sea." Michael said.

Tears began to roll down her cheeks.

Just then the doctor approached to tell them how Bridget was doing.

"Sorry for the wait. It seems that Bridget may have an anaplastic astrocytoma, which is essentially a malignant brain tumor."

"You said may have. You're not sure?" Michael asked.

"We are pretty sure this is what she has from the MRI, but we will have to perform a tissue biopsy to have a more definitive diagnosis. We have one scheduled for tomorrow morning. In the meantime, we will keep her on seizure medication and sedatives. These should help keep her brain from firing too much, which is causing her seizures and headaches. You may go see her if you would like, but we gave her a mild sedative, so she may be a little out of it. Don't stay for too long—she will need her rest."

"Thank you, doctor." Michael said, as the doctor walked away.

"We will wait here. You go in first Sea."

"Thank you, Michael. I won't be long." Sea said, as she walked away.

Sea was thankful the doctor had interrupted. She was able to avoid the truth once again.

"Hey, Bridget, how are you feeling?"

"Okay."

"I'm so sorry about the news. How are you holding up?"

"It's not easy. I'm scared, but there is hope. The doctors will know more tomorrow. You know Sea, as I've been sitting here waiting for the results, I've been thinking about you and Mitch. You need to tell him your secret before it's too late. As I've just discovered, life is short and you need to make the most of it while you can. Don't go on living in fear, it drains you of all happiness. Mitch might surprise you. He loves you. You need to tell him, dear."

"Michael said the same thing to me a few minutes ago."

"That's because we know when enough is enough."

"Why is everyone pressuring me about this?" Sea snapped. "I'm not ready. I can't deal with his rejection and your illness all at the same time."

"You're using me as an excuse?"

"No..." Sea thought about it for a minute and said, "I'm not going to promise anything, but I'll think about telling him."

"Thank you, Sea. That's all I'm asking."

After a few minutes, Bridget fell asleep.

Sea went to tell Michael and Mitch that Bridget was sleeping and that there was nothing else they could do today.

Sea called Sarah and her father, to let them know that Bridget was in the hospital. Mr. Gallagher and his daughter would fly into Bradley airport later that night. Michael offered to pick them up.

The next day, everyone decided to meet for breakfast before the biopsy was scheduled. Sarah was thrilled to finally meet Mitch. She talked his ear off all through breakfast. Mr. Gallagher and Michael talked about the old days. Sea watched the others converse. She picked at her food but didn't eat much. She was too nervous. She had made a promise to Bridget. She decided that the sooner she told him, the better. She was tired of torturing herself and him. When they were finished with breakfast, Sea took Mitch to the side and asked him if he would meet her in the hospital cafeteria at ten o'clock to talk, an hour before the biopsy. He agreed.

*

"Thanks for meeting me, Mitch. I ordered you a coffee."

"Thanks..."

There was an awkward silence between them.

"I'm really worried about Bridget." Mitch looked intently into her eyes with concern.

"I know. I'm praying the doctors are wrong and the biopsy is negative." Sea returned his gaze.

"I don't think it will be. It may explain why she has been so peculiar lately."

"Yeah. You might be right. Your father must be going through a lot too."

"He's having a very hard time with it. He loves her."

"I was surprised you agreed to talk."

Mitch thought about it for a minute. "I'm curious... and I'm willing to put my feelings aside because of what your family is going through."

Sea looked at her hands, resting in her lap. "Your dad and my aunt seem to think it's time I tell you everything."

"They're right. You should have told me a long time ago."

"I know. I know."

"Why now? What's changed?"

"Bridget's tumor. I shouldn't waste any more time. Time is more precious than we think it is. I don't want to lose you forever and the only way I can think of to reconcile, is to tell you the truth. I have to grow up. I have to face my fears and deal with whatever happens next, the best way I can. It can't be any worse than it is right now with you hating me." Sea took a deep breath to calm herself. "I never meant to hurt you Mitch. I've been so afraid to tell you everything. I know I should have trusted you."

Sea paused.

"My ex-fiancé broke our engagement because I'm not able to have children."

Mitch thought a moment. "Where you born that way or did something happen?"

"I was shot in the abdomen by a man, who minutes before, shot his wife in the head for cheating on him."

"Really? You were?" he said surprised. "Where were you when it happened?"

"I was in a wedding gown shop minding my own business, when at the same instance, this man decided to seek revenge on his wife. I was in the wrong place at the wrong time."

"That's awful. I'm so sorry to hear that. It happens so often now. It's one of the plagues of the twenty-first century—mindless shootings."

"It is like an epidemic. Dumb people keep catching the fever," she said.

"Where exactly were you shot?" Mitch asked.

"The bullet ripped through my intestines and mangled my uterus. My uterus was not salvageable. My ovaries are still intact, so I'd be able to use a surrogate but that's very expensive."

"That sounds difficult to recover from. I'm sorry you had to go through that."

Sea was silent for a moment, absorbing his empathy. "It was extremely traumatic for me. I was in the hospital for two weeks. And then my fiancé dumped me when he heard I wouldn't be able to carry on his bloodline. He said he didn't want to spend the time, energy and money it would take to have a child through a surrogate. And of course, he didn't want to adopt—nothing less than carrying on the bloodline was acceptable to his family."

"I broke up with you because I couldn't subject you to a life of childlessness or having to spend all your money on surrogacy. But, above all, I didn't want to risk having you reject me. I wanted to tell you but my heart wasn't strong enough to take another blow."

"You should have trusted me, Sea." he declared. "I wouldn't have gone anywhere."

"I know." she said. "I was blinded by fear. All I could envision was the same reaction my fiancé had. I'm sorry."

"Your ex-fiancé is not me." Mitch chided.

"You're right. You're not. You're ten times better. I hope someday you'll be able to have faith in me again. We could start from scratch, when you're ready." she said.

"I don't know, Sea. Maybe. Let me think about it."

"That's all I'm asking."

"We should go back. Bridget leaves soon for her biopsy and I want to see her before she goes in." Mitch said.

As they walked back to Bridget's room she said, "I didn't want you to settle for me. You deserve to have a family of your own. I didn't think you would be happy living the life I could give you."

Mitch listened, but didn't respond.

CHAPTER NINETEEN

"Are you comfortable Aunt Bridget?" Sea asked, as she fluffed up her pillow.

"Yes, that's much better. Thank you, sweetie."

"How does your head feel?"

"It hurts a little but they have me on some nice pain killers to help with that." Bridget said, as she tucked her hair under the wrap the doctors had around her head to protect from infections.

Two hours later, the doctor came in to tell her that the biopsy had come back positive. She in fact did have an anaplastic astrocytoma, a rare, grade III malignant brain tumor.

Sea asked the doctor, "When will she start radiation and chemotherapy?"

"Well, first, she needs to have surgery. We need to go in and try to remove the tumor. It will be an extensive surgery. The tumor will be difficult to remove. This type of tumor has many arms extending and attaching to surrounding tissue, making it difficult to remove completely. Once we get as much as we can, we will follow up with radiation."

"I see. Thank you, doctor."

"I'm so sorry you have to go through this Aunt Bridget, but I will be here to help you in any way I can."

"Thank you, dear. I'm glad you decided to move up here. It's been great having you around, especially now when I really need someone."

"I'm glad you were willing to take me in."

"Have you talked to Mitch yet?" Bridget asked.

"Yes, I told him everything. I'm not sure he'll ever want to get back together though." Sea said, as tears started to fall. "I really messed things up!" she cried. "I should have told him everything from the beginning."

"Be patient. He will come around. I know he still loves you. His pride stops him."

"I hope you're right." Sea wiped her eyes and blew her nose. "When's the surgery?"

"In two days. They want to give me enough time to get my affairs in order because of the risks involved. My lawyer is coming later today to help me with that."

"I'm going to grab some coffee. I'll be back soon." Sea said. She didn't want to be away from her aunt for long. She wanted to spend as much time with her as she could before her surgery.

Two days later, Bridget underwent brain surgery. The surgery lasted only three hours. When the neurosurgeon made his way to the tumor, he could tell that it was going to be difficult to remove. The tumor had an extensive vascular supply and was embedded more than he had anticipated. Once he started cutting into it, a devastating chain reaction occurred. The surgical team couldn't control the bleeding and Bridget's blood pressure started to drop. Bridget's brain and heart couldn't handle the stress, and she died on the table. The doctors were very apologetic and said that these things happen, especially with this type of tumor. The tumor was twisted and entwined with surrounding tissue so extensively that Bridget hadn't had much of a chance.

Everyone was in shock. Everything happened so fast. There was some peace of mind, in that everyone was able to wish her well before the surgery. Mr. Gallagher arranged the funeral. A few days after Bridget's death, her lawyer informed Sea that Bridget had left the house to her. Bridget didn't have any children of her own so she had left most of her money and belongings with Sea. She had wanted a few personal items to go to her brother, Michael and Mitch.

Bridget's service was a week after her death. Mr. Gallagher and Sarah were already in Massachusetts. Mrs. Gallagher flew in from Maryland, and Tommy and Molly attended the service. Mr. Stone stayed home to care for the children.

At her funeral, Michael gave a tearful eulogy. Afterwards, her brother thanked him for his kind words. The reception was held at Bridget's home and all her loved ones and friends talked about how Bridget had influenced them and their lives. Bridget had the kindest soul. She looked after Mitch when his mother, her best friend, passed away. She was a friend and confidant for Michael. She was willing and able to help Sea when she needed a place to stay. Bridget will be missed.

"Sea." She turned around and saw Mitch standing there.

"Mitch," she said. "Is everything okay?"

"No, it's not. I can't stop thinking about the last words Bridget said to me. She wanted me to make things right with you, to forgive you. I'm not sure that I can. It will take time."

Sea winced at his words. "I understand." She was resigning herself to the fact that they would never get back together.

"Thanks for apologizing to Molly. She told me you two had talked and are actually friends now. That was really good of you Sea."

"I'm not a total monster." Sea said jokingly. "I'm only human and I do care. We can at least be friends for now, can't we? I'm sure Bridget would be pleased with that."

"Yes. I have no problem with us being friends." Mitch said. "How are you holding up?" he asked her.

"I'm doing okay." Sea answered. "I miss my aunt deeply. She was a great friend to me this past year. I'm glad I moved up here and got to know her better before she passed."

"I'm sure." he said.

"How are you doing, Mitch? You two were close as well."

"I think it would have been tougher if I had been younger. It helped to have her in my life growing up. I will miss her delightful company... and her home-cooked meals."

Sarah, watching them from a distance, wondered if they were getting back together. She joined them.

"Hi!" she said. "It was a great service, don't you think?"

"Yes. It was." Mitch said.

"Your father did a great job with the eulogy." Sarah commented.

"Thanks. He really loved your aunt. They were really great friends. Please excuse me. I wanted to talk to a few other people before I leave." Mitch started to walk away.

"Oh wait!" Sarah called after him. "Some of us are meeting at the pub later. Do you want to come?"

"Sure… why not. Which one?" he called to her.

"Sea will text you the information." Sarah said.

"Okay." Mitch said from across the room.

"So… are you two back together?" Sarah asked with anticipation.

"No. He said that he's not ready to forgive me and only wants to be friends. Aunt Bridget's dying wish was for him to forgive me and he can't do it. I need a drink." Sea walked to the wine bar to pour herself a glass. Suddenly, Molly was beside her.

"Don't!" Molly exclaimed, as she moved her hand over the glass.

Sea frowned and said, "Why? I'm old enough to have a drink. I'm going to pour myself a glass thank you very much."

"I have a plan."

"What? What do you mean? What kind of plan?" Then it dawned on her. "Oh. Don't bother. He won't forgive me."

"It wouldn't hurt to try. I know he still loves you."

Sea sighed.

"So… what's your big idea?"

"I want you to be a designated driver tonight. Tommy and I both think Mitch will be drinking a little too much tonight because of Bridget and… well… you. My plan is for you to be sober so you can help him home later. Your father is not drinking as well, to help any one of us. What do you think?"

"I think you're crazy. And what am I supposed to do once I get him home—seduce him?"

"Maybe not seduce per se, but help him into the apartment and see what happens next. Mitch's defenses are down when he drinks. Tell him how much you love him. Make sure you dress sexy tonight too. Guys have a hard time resisting when they are intoxicated."

"Fine. I won't drink. I hope I don't regret this." Sea said.

*

Later that night, Sarah, Sea, Molly, Tommy, Mr. Gallagher and Mitch gathered at one of the local pubs. When Mitch first arrived, he gulped down two shots of whiskey and ordered a beer. Molly gave Sea a look of "told you so."

Sea wore skinny jeans and a pretty blue shirt that brought out the color of her hair. Mitch watched Sea, but only when she wasn't looking. Out of the corner of her eye, Sea noticed that he was staring at her. He did it several times throughout the night—it gave her some hope. At one point, Sea and Sarah played Tommy and Mitch a game of pool. It was the only time that Mitch interacted with her. After a few hours, they called it a night.

"Who's designated driver Tommy?" Mitch asked.

"Mr. Gallagher and Sea are." Tommy answered.

"I'll take you home Mitch." Mr. Gallagher offered.

"No. I got it, Dad. Thanks," Sea quickly cut in. "Besides, I know where he lives."

Mitch smiled when he heard this.

"Oh great, it's raining out." Molly said sarcastically as Tommy was holding the door open for her.

Mr. Gallagher and Mitch stayed inside while Sea went to get her car. Mitch was not going to move very quickly in his condition. Once Sea pulled up to the front, Mr. Gallagher helped Mitch into the car. Sea didn't know what to say the moment they were alone.

"You looked really nice tonight, Sea. I like that blue shirt on you. You should wear it more often."

"Thanks."

Two minutes later.

"Oh no. Stop the car!"

"What's wrong?"

"I think I'm gonna barf. Hurry!"

As soon as she was able, Sea pulled over onto the shoulder. Mitch opened the door, leaned out and vomited all over the ground. A few seconds later, he did it again. He was soaked through from the pouring rain. Sea had to lean over him to shut the door. Mitch was too drunk to do it himself. When she did, her hair got soaked. Mitch laughed at her.

"I love your hair like that. It's beautiful." He chuckled.

"You're hilarious." Sea said, as she put her seatbelt back on and pulled out onto the road.

It was cold and almost freezing. She was surprised it wasn't snowing. The roads were getting slick so she drove slowly. It took a while to get him home. When she finally did, she had to help him up the stairs and into his apartment. Now they were both soaking wet.

She brought him to the bathroom and turned the shower on, and started undressing him.

"What're you doing?" he asked, alarmed.

"I'm helping you out of your clothes. You will catch pneumonia in those. I'm going to put you in the shower to warm you up. I need to warm up too."

"You're taking off your clothes?"

"Most of them. I'm leaving my underwear on, yours too. This is already awkward enough, but I don't want you to get sick."

Mitch watched her as she undressed him and herself. As Sea helped him into the shower, he said, "You would make a great mother."

As he sat in the shower with her, Sea began to cry uncontrollably.

"Are you okay? What did I say?" Mitch asked, as he watched her cry.

"You didn't say anything. Everything seems to be hitting me all at once. Bridget dying.. Hurting you and feeling like I've lost you forever. Mad at myself for all the stupid things I've said and done since we broke up. And even if we were to get back together, the thought of not being able to give you children of your own—hurts so much. I'm overwhelmed."

Mitch had sobered up a little since he vomited. He gathered water in his mouth from the water stream to remove the bad taste. When he finished, he slowly stroked her cheek with his finger. She stopped crying. They looked at each other.

Sea dried off with a towel and then helped Mitch up. While he finished drying off, Sea put their wet clothes in the dryer. She picked out a shirt and shorts from his dresser to wear while her clothes were drying.

"Are you going to spend the night?" he asked.

"I wasn't planning to. I was going to leave after my clothes dried." Sea answered.

"Aren't they going to get wet again when you go outside? It may rain all night. You can stay the night if you want."

"Are you sure? I didn't want to impose."

"It's fine. The roads are pretty nasty too. I wouldn't want anything to happen to you."

There was silence in the room after he said this. Sea didn't know what to say.

"You can have the bed. I'll sleep on the couch." Mitch offered.

"Okay. Thanks." she said, as she went to get sheets.

"Sea?"

"Yes." she said, as she turned around from making up the couch for him.

Mitch hesitated.

"Yes?"

No answer.

"Mitch, what is it?" she insisted.

He hesitated a few more seconds then said, "I forgive you."

Sea was stunned. She never thought she would ever hear those words uttered.

"Do you mean it? Are you saying that because of what Bridget said?"

"Partly, but I do mean it. I wouldn't say it if I didn't mean it."

Sea stopped what she was doing and sat down on the couch.

"So what does this mean?" she asked him.

"It means… I'm willing to start over, if you are." he answered.

"Yes. I'd really like that. Are you sure?"

"No, but I'm willing to give you a second chance. Everyone deserves a second chance. I don't want to see you suffer any more. I think you've suffered enough in life. I've been hurt. You've been hurt. It's time to put away our fears and start fresh.

"I'm sure this is not easy for you."

"No. It's not," he said. "But no matter how hard I tried, I couldn't stop thinking about you."

"May I hug you?" Sea asked.

"Yes. I'd like that," Mitch answered.

Sea slowly walked over and gave him a hug. She was so happy to finally feel his embrace. She had wondered for a long time if she would ever feel his arms around her again. She didn't want it to end. Mitch moved back a little to face her and her head whipped up to register what was happening.

"What is it Mitch?" Sea said, as she looked at him intensely.

"Well… I was going to kiss you, but I have vomit breath and you have raccoon eyes."

Sea quickly shoved him back to go look in the mirror. She was mortified.

"Why didn't you tell me sooner?"

"I didn't want to hurt your feelings. But, I had to say something, I didn't want to start laughing and kill the mood."

"Too late for that." she said, as she tried to get it off with regular soap. She didn't have her eye makeup remover and thus had a tough time removing it.

Mitch came up behind her and said, "You're still beautiful to me." He then gave her a hug and kissed her on the cheek. Sea responded with a smile and nuzzled his neck.

"What made you change your mind about forgiving me?"

"You've opened up more in the last two weeks than the whole time we were dating. You finally told me your big secret. When you took your clothes off, I knew then how much you trusted me—to be that vulnerable is not easy."

"Do you want to share the bed with me? You don't have to sleep on the couch." she said.

"I'd like that."

CHAPTER TWENTY

"Good morning sleepy head. How are you feeling?" Sea asked Mitch.

"Not so good. My head is killing me."

"I'll get you some water." When she returned, she said, "I wish Bridget could have seen us back together."

"I think she knows," Mitch said.

"I hope so."

"I miss her," he said.

"I miss her too. It all happened so fast. It was way too soon."

"How's your dad doing?" Sea asked.

"I'm not sure. I'm going to see him later today and find out."

"Good. I'm going to have lunch with Dad and Sarah before they fly back to Maryland. I'd better get a move on. Are you going to be okay?"

"Yeah. I'll be fine. I think I'll sleep a little more before I get up."

"Okay. I'll see you later." Sea gave him a kiss on the lips and left.

*

When Sea arrived home, she saw someone sitting on her steps. She couldn't make out who it was from a distance. The man walked up to her car when she put it in park.

Sea opened her car door and said, "What are you doing here?"

"I've come to ask you back. It's fine you can't have kids. I changed my mind. I don't want kids after all."

"Trevor… it's been over a year. I've moved on."

"I don't understand. I'm willing to take you back. Not many guys would want to marry someone who can't reproduce, but I do."

"Why? What's changed? You were so sure before that you wanted kids of your own and now it's no big deal. I don't buy it. What happened?"

"My fiancé made me get a fertility test before our wedding. She was adamant about having kids, like I was, and when I got the results, I found out that I was sterile. My fiancé dumped me the same day."

"It doesn't feel good, does it?" she asked.

"No. It doesn't." he answered.

"Didn't take you long to find someone else."

"My mother was pressuring me to get married. She won't stop talking about grandchildren."

"I'm sorry about your predicament, but I've moved on. I found someone who truly cares about me. He doesn't mind the road less traveled."

"Are you sure? I'm not going to offer again," he demanded.

"I'm sure. I think you better leave now. I don't want you here."

Stung, Trevor turned on his heel, and walked away. Sea never saw him again.

*

After Sea dropped her dad and sister off at the airport, she went to Molly's place.

"So how did it go?" Molly asked, anxious for a response.

"Better than expected."

"What does that mean? Don't hold me in suspense. What happened?"

"He forgave me and we made up. We are going to start from scratch. Re-establish our relationship, which is fine with me because I'm just happy to have him back."

"How are you and Tommy doing?"

"Really well. I think I love him, Sea. He makes me so happy. He actually made me breakfast this morning. Can you imagine Tommy cooking?"

Sea laughed. "No. I can't."

"Well he does and he did. I couldn't believe it. He didn't seem the type."

"I know. Doesn't sound like the Tommy I know, but love can do strange things to you, it seems."

They both laughed.

"I'm really glad we're friends, Molly. Thanks for helping me get back with Mitch. I never thought he would forgive me."

"You're most welcome! When you're in love you want others

around you to be in love too. It makes it all sweeter. Plus, it was so obvious how he felt about you. He never looked at me, the way he looked at you. That's why I couldn't help myself with Tommy. He adores me and no one has ever made me feel that way before."

"Well, you deserve it. You have a beautiful soul Molly."

"Thank you!" Molly said, as she gave her a hug.

CHAPTER TWENTY-ONE

Four months after Bridget had passed away, Sea and Mitch moved in together. One afternoon, as they enjoyed a freshly brewed cup of coffee, they chatted about Molly's pregnancy and engagement to Tommy. Seeing Molly's round belly tugged at Sea's heart. She desperately wanted to bring a child into being. Suddenly, they heard a knock at the door. Mitch went to find out who it was. When he opened the door, he saw a woman standing there with a baby in her arms. She didn't look well.

"Hello. May I help you?" Mitch asked.

"I really hope so," she responded. "Is your name Michael Anderson Jr?"

"Yes it is," he replied a little warily.

"My name is Dorothy Woods and this here is Samuel. He's… your son."

"My son? How on earth do you figure that?"

"My wife and I picked your sperm when we decided to have kids. You donated sperm correct?"

"Yes, but that was like five years ago. It's still good after that long?"

"Apparently it is."

"Well… what can I do for you?" he asked.

Sea could hear part of the conversation from the kitchen and went to see who he was talking to.

"Hello," Sea said, as she reached the door. "Did you say that this baby is his?"

"Yes I did," the woman said. "My partner and I chose his semen donation."

"Please, do come in." Sea instructed. "My name is Sea, like the ocean, and this is my boyfriend, Mitch."

"My birth name is Michael Anderson Jr., but everyone calls me Mitch."

"Thank you, Mitch. It's nice to meet you both. As I was telling you earlier, my name is Dorothy and this is Samuel."

"Have a seat on the couch, Dorothy," Sea offered.

"Thank you. You have a lovely home, Sea."

"Thanks. My aunt left it to me. Can I get you something to drink?"

"Yes. That would be nice. I'd love some water please."

Mitch waited until Sea was back with the water before he continued to question her.

"Here you go." Sea said.

"Thank you. You're very kind."

Mitch couldn't wait for her to drink the water. "Why are you here?" he said dumbfounded.

Dorothy took a sip of water before she started. "My wife died three months ago in a car accident and a week ago I was diagnosed with stage four pancreatic cancer. I'm looking for someone to care for our child. Our families disowned us and I don't want him to go to a foster home. I thought you might consider taking him, since you're the birth father."

"How did you find me?" Mitch said, still in shock.

"It wasn't easy, but a few people were willing to bend the rules because of my dire situation."

"How old is he?" Sea asked.

"He's three months old." Dorothy replied. "Do you want to hold him?"

"I would love to," she said with excitement. "Which one of you gave birth?"

"My partner did. She always wanted to have a baby. Me on the other hand, not so much. I don't do well with pain."

"That means she must have passed away shortly after giving birth?" Mitch observed.

"She did. Two weeks after he was born, a teenager running a red light hit her car. Samuel wasn't in the car with her–he was home with me."

"I know this is quite a shock to you both, but I'm getting weaker by the day and I was hoping for an answer as soon as possible. If you're not able to do it, I have to find someone who can, before I get too weak."

"Of course we will take him in. Right, Mitch?"

"Will you excuse us for a moment? I need to speak to Sea in

private."

"Of course. No problem."

Mitch led Sea to the kitchen.

"I can't take care of a baby, I have a job. We aren't even married. We've only been living together for two months."

"Slow down Mitch. Take a breath." Sea said in a hushed voice. "We can do this. This is a miracle in disguise. You will get to have a child of your own. I will quit my job while you work. You make enough money for the both of us."

Sea let him sit with it for a moment.

"Are you sure you'd be willing to do that Sea? It's a big responsibility."

"Yes I'm sure. I love you. I want you to be happy. We could have a family. Something I never thought we could have. It will make your dad so happy to be a grandfather. Also, I think his mom should stay here. We have the room" Sea said. "She can help take care of him until she is too weak to. She shouldn't live on her own without him. It wouldn't be right. She will want to be with him until the end."

"I was thinking the same thing. It's the least we could do after giving us such a beautiful gift."

They returned to the living room to give Dorothy the good news.

"Yes. We will take him in." Mitch said. "And you can stay here as well."

"Oh, thank you so much. I really appreciate this." Dorothy said.

"Thank you! You're giving us such a precious gift. You can sleep in the downstairs bedroom so you don't have to climb the stairs. He will sleep in his crib next to you until you need us to take over. We want everything to run as smoothly as possible for you." Sea said.

Dorothy gasped. Sea turned around to see what Dorothy was looking at. Mitch was on one knee.

"Sea. I love you too. Will you marry me?" he asked.

Sea's hands covered her mouth. She was in shock.

"Yes. I will marry you."

Dorothy beamed as she watched them.

Mitch placed a ring on Sea's finger.

"Where did you get that? You planned this?"

"No. Not for today. A few months from now, maybe. It's my mother's wedding ring. My dad gave it to me the day after we got back together. Remember I told you we were meeting. After I told him we were together again, he knew it was the perfect time to give me the ring."

"May I hold Samuel again?" Sea asked.

"Of course. Here." Dorothy held the baby up for Sea.

Sea looked lovingly into Samuel's eyes and said, "You are so handsome Samuel, just like your father. This is the best day of my life."

Catherine Elizabeth Lambert

ABOUT THE AUTHOR

Catherine Lambert is forty-three and she and her husband have been married for over twenty-four years. They live on the outskirts of Washington D.C. This is Catherine's second book; her first book, a memoir, was self-published in 2011 titled, "Lost in a Sea of Mothers: Am I a Mother Yet?.

Made in the USA
Middletown, DE
29 December 2015